The Fire
Brand

D0812948

Jennifer Rees

The Fire Brand

Marshall Pickering

Copyright © 1980 Jennifer Rees
First published 1982
by Pickering & Inglis Ltd
34–42 Cleveland Street, London WIP 5FB

ISBN 0 7208 2313 7

To Sarah Jane,
my foster daughter

Photoset in Great Britain by
Rowland Phototypesetting Ltd
Bury St Edmunds, Suffolk
and printed by Richard Clay Ltd
Bungay, Suffolk

Contents

Is not this a brand
plucked out of the fire?
                    —*Zechariah 3:2*

1

The Last Chance

"This is your very last chance, Jake. If you don't make a go of it here, you'll finish up in a detention home."

Jake, sitting stubbornly alone in the back seat, looked at the social worker's fat, white hands on the steering wheel and hated him.

"It's this new young man, who's been put in charge of our department," continued Mr Lewis. "He wants to give you this last chance in another foster home, but it's against my advice."

I'll kill you one day! thought Jake. But I'll do it slowly and painfully. Some people have decent social workers. Just my luck to get lumbered with you. You've always hated me, ever since I bit your thumb when I was small. I'd bite it off now if I had the chance.

"You've acted like a vandal and a thief," went on the case worker, "but you've got a chance to start again in a village where no one knows you. You're a very lucky boy."

Charming! thought Jake. Everyone hates me guts; no one can get rid of me fast enough; and he says I'm a lucky boy!

"These people who are willing to take you," continued Mr Lewis, "have had quite a lot of success with difficult cases, and they live right out in the country, which may help."

Jake scowled and thought, They'll wish they didn't live anywhere soon. Here's one difficult case they'll be sorry they took.

He remembered the first time Mr Lewis had driven him to a foster home. That was seven years ago, when he was only five. He cried all the way because he didn't want to leave the children's home, where he had lived all his life. He liked the foster home when he got there, and for two years he'd been as good as he knew how to be. Then the father had gone off and left the mother. She said it was the strain of fostering someone else's child that had broken up the home, so Jake was sent to another children's home.

After that, it didn't seem worthwhile trying to be good. No sooner did he get to like the staff in the home, but they would leave, or have a nervous breakdown. The other children kept being transferred or fostered out, so there was no point in getting friendly with them either. Mr Lewis had tried several other foster homes, but Jake figured he'd just be rejected again. So he was as difficult as he could be, just to see how long they would stand him.

About that time he started lighting a match to things. Burning that classroom down had been great. But the Youth Club building was even better! That was when he'd got the nickname Fire Brand. He had lived in so many places now, a detention home wouldn't be that much worse.

They had turned off the motorway long since and were now winding through country lanes. From his seclusion in the back seat, Jake surveyed the scenery with disgust. Nothing but fields, hills, and woods. Whatever did people do with themselves out here?

"Tidy yourself up a bit," said Mr Lewis fussily. "We're nearly there."

Jake looked at his reflection in the car mirror. He had inherited his Nigerian father's crinkly black hair and his Irish mother's white skin, but right across the side of his face was a bright red birthmark, giving him a grotesque appearance.

All his life he had been plagued by the riddle which goes, "What is black and white and red all over?" The answer was, "Not a newspaper – but Jake!" Everyone who made that joke thought he was the first to think of it. Jake had broken a boy's arm for saying that once too often.

"Here's the village now," said Mr Lewis. Jake didn't want to see the beautiful old houses grouped around the village square, or the ancient church and quaint little shops, so he closed his eyes and planned his strategy.

Shall I do something really big to terrify these people right away? he thought. Or start small and work up slowly? As they turned down a pretty lane, he decided not to speak at all.

They'll try and be all friendly at first, so if I keeps me mouth shut it'll rile them, he thought grimly.

The house, when they reached it, looked as if it was made of cardboard, surrounded by a garden resembling a rubbish heap.

This hole'll burn nicely, thought Jake with satisfaction. It'll be me last job around here.

The untidy house seemed full of people trying to be friendly, and the smell of frying onions. The foster mother, who was as fat as a barrel, didn't seem

9

worried by Jake's silent stare, as she hurried about getting the tea. Her husband was a little fellow whom, Jake felt, would give no trouble. But their son Peter was another matter.

He's bigger than me, thought Jake. I'll have to watch him.

There was a younger girl whom Jake felt he could kick around easily. When they sat down to tea, she stared so fixedly at his birthmark that Jake felt he could cheerfully strangle her.

He had half decided not to eat anything, but the plateful of food that was placed before him looked so good, he'd had three helpings before he could stop himself.

"I'll see you soon," said Mr Lewis, waving as he left.

Too right! thought Jake, with a mouthful. But they'll be taking me away from here in a smart police car, not your old banger.

"I expect you'd like to see your room now, Jake," said the fat woman. "We've converted the attic for you."

That's right, stick me up with the rats, and the cobwebs, thought Jake, following her shaking bulk up the narrow stairs. When he reached the attic room he was pleasantly surprised, in spite of himself.

"We've left the walls blank, so that you can put up your own posters. You can do what you like up here. No one will come in unless you invite them."

Never in all his twelve years had Jake had a room to himself. His own private world.

I'll give meself a break for a couple of weeks, he thought, bouncing on the soft bed. I won't do anything too big, so they send me away before I've had time to enjoy all this.

He lay on his bed, enjoying the peace, until someone called him down for cheese sandwiches and hot chocolate. There wasn't a children's home anywhere with service like this.

"You'll be coming with me to school tomorrow," said Peter, bursting into Jake's pleasant thought. "We have to go about five miles on the school bus, but it's quite good when you get there. It's small for a comprehensive school, only about six hundred pupils. And the teachers aren't bad."

Jake had never met a teacher who was "not bad." In fact, no teacher ever came close. They had all appeared to hate him as much as he hated them. But he'd given as good as he got! He knew for certain that he had caused three nervous breakdowns. And five teachers gave up and found other jobs. He had been to seven different schools and managed to learn nothing at all from them.

"We wear uniforms. My old blazer should do you, and you can wear my spare tie until you get your own stuff."

Keep your own fleas! thought Jake, and went up the stairs to bed.

Jake had never been a good sleeper. To lie all night without being disturbed by someone else's tossing or snores was one of the best things that had ever happened to him.

When he woke up, he deliberately put on his oldest jeans and his holeyest shirt.

Let them try and make me put on school gear, he thought with relish. But everyone was too busy consuming a wonderful breakfast of bacon and eggs to notice what he was wearing.

"Dad's a postman," said the little girl. "That's why he's not here." Jake could not have cared less where the silly little man was, and spread marmalade thickly on his toast.

"Here're your sandwiches, boys," said the Jelly Mountain, as Jake had silently christened Mrs Jarvis. "I'll cook a big dinner in the evening for you," she explained to Jake.

"If you wear a blazer and tie, like everybody else, people won't pick on you so much at school," warned Peter, stuffing homework into his school bag with the sandwiches. But when Jake didn't answer, he said no more and they set off together up the lane.

I hate him! thought Jake as they hurried for the bus. I'll get that grin off his face before I'm through.

It was just the same as every other school. Jake felt the same trapped feeling as the doors closed behind him. The same old smell – disinfectant, smelly feet, and boiling cabbage. And the usual startled faces gazing at his birthmark, then the same sniggers and whispers.

"This is Mr Percy," said the Headmaster. "He's in charge of the Remedial Department, where you will be for the time being."

Shoved away with the Thickies, thought Jake as he waited tensely for the inevitable question. It came soon after the Headmaster had left.

"Can you read?" asked the teacher, and Jake felt the eyes of the class fixed upon him. Deliberately he rolled his eyes, let his mouth hang open, and made a gobbling sound in his throat.

"Yes, well –" said the teacher, hastily, "don't worry about it. Suppose you come over here and paint me a nice picture."

That worked all right, thought Jake, with satisfaction. He won't make me do any work now.

But he had no intention of playing the idiot outside the classroom. When the bell rang in mid-morning, he followed the crowd out into the fresh air.

He knew what would happen now, and he flexed his muscles and waited. Sure enough, he was soon surrounded by a sea of jeering faces.

"Did your mother spill red paint over your poor little facey, did she?" cooed a fat boy in glasses.

"Where did you get your hair curled?" shouted someone else, while a red-headed boy in a brand-new blazer picked at Jake's old shirt and snickered, "Had moths, did you?"

Jake took it in stony silence, until the "black and white and red all over" joke came out. Then he had had enough. He punched three noses and dealt out a black eye before anyone knew what happened.

"The worm's turned!" shouted the fat boy in delight. But none of them could do much against Jake's right hook. When the bell rang they melted thankfully away, leaving the fat boy groping about for his glasses and the redhead moaning and groaning.

After that, everyone left Jake alone, both staff and pupils. But that was the way it always was for Jake.

The whole family was sitting around the table when Jake and Peter got in that evening. The smell of the food that the Jelly Mountain heaped onto their plates was indescribably delicious.

Jake was waiting for remarks and questions about his cuts and bruises, but Mrs Jarvis only asked pleasantly, "How did it go?"

Jake scowled and shrugged, but Peter grinned at him across the table.

"I saw you with that crowd from the second year," Peter said. "You were great, really. That's the only way to deal with heels like that. I'd have come out to give you a hand but I was stuck in a French lesson."

Jake glanced at the postman. One of his foster fathers had taken a strap to the boys for fighting, but the little man did not appear to be listening. So Jake had another piece of apple pie and felt happier than he had all day.

2

Campaign of Hate

It was the middle of the first Saturday morning. Jake was lying on his bed wondering what ever you did in the country at weekends. Peter had gone off on his bike and the girl was watching TV. The Jelly Mountain was busy in the kitchen, judging by the smells.

I could do with a smoke, thought Jake idly, but I'm broke. I'll just sneak down while they're all busy and see if I can find that fatty's purse. She might be good for a little cash.

The handbag was hanging on the hook with her enormous coat, at the dark end of the long narrow hall. He had to fight his way through piles of boots, shopping bags, old toys, and dogs' dishes to reach it, but the note-case inside the bag was as fat as its owner.

"Jake!" called a voice behind him. Jake froze – his hand still in the bag. Mr Jarvis closed the front door at the end of the hall and took off his postman's cap and jacket.

Now what? thought Jake as he slowly let his hand drop to his side. But the little man was whistling happily as he walked up the hall to hang his things by his wife's coat. Jake began to feel confused and irritated. Was this man so thick that he did not realise what had been happening, or was he too afraid to say anything?

"I'm going to clear the garden up a bit today, Jake," he said at last. "I need someone to make a bonfire of all our old rubbish. Would you do that, do you think?"

Much as Jake would have liked to refuse, bonfires were his ruling passion. He found himself nodding instead. The rest of the day passed blissfully for Jake as he burned an enormous quantity of junk from the garden shed, back porch, and greenhouse.

What a messy lot they are to collect all this stuff, he thought. But as the flames leaped up, he was filled with the sheer ecstasy that fire always gave him. It was dusk before they had finished, and Jake could not remember enjoying a day so much for a long, long time.

The next day was Sunday and, as they ate hot rolls and yellow honey for breakfast, Jake realised the others were wearing their best clothes.

"We go to church on Sunday, Jake," explained Mrs Jarvis. "Would you like to come too?"

Jake nearly shook his head off. He was terrified of churches. A woman who worked in one of his many children's homes had told him that God punished wicked boys and that he would end up in hell fire.

Hell he did not mind, because he loved fire, but God was another matter.

"We don't go to the big one with the steeple," explained the little girl, Janie. "Just to the green tin one, along the lane. It's ever such fun."

An angry God could live in green tin, just as surely as under a steeple, so Jake scowled and shook his head again.

Typical of them to barge off to church all dressed up in their best, he thought sourly as he watched them disappear up the lane.

The endless morning stretched before him and, just for the sake of something to do, he went out to explore the village. As it turned out, he enjoyed himself. He earmarked three haystacks, a scout hut, and an old timbered barn, any of which could easily be ignited if life in Streetfield became too boring.

Wherever he went, he found the village totally quiet and deserted that sleepy Sunday morning. To the city boy, the silence was eery and uncanny. So it was with relief that he heard in the distance the sound of a crowd of cheerful-sounding people. He hurried eagerly around the corner, wondering what could be going on. He found himself in the crowd, as they stood talking and laughing in the lane. Too late he realised he was in the middle of the congregation departing from the little green church.

Looking around wildly for escape, he spotted Mrs Jarvis, bulging under her tight best dress. She was talking to a tall red-necked woman, who immediately fixed Jake with a threatening glare, and said, "So this is your latest Little Problem, Mrs Jarvis." Advancing upon Jake she continued patronisingly, "You're a lucky boy to be allowed to live in a nice village like this. I hope you're going to behave yourself."

Jake's answer was so obscene that it could not be printed, and during the stunned silence that followed, he escaped down the lane.

When he reached the safety of the empty house, he wondered what the Jarvises would do when they returned. He could remember a most violent occasion when he had been forced to apologise to a foster mother's aunt for using a similar set of words; but the very idea of this odd little postman trying to force him to do anything was laughable. He waited for them in the untidy sitting room, his hands clenched, ready for battle to commence.

But when this extraordinary family returned, they seemed unable to speak at all, they just rolled around their sitting room, helpless with laughter.

"Oh, Mum," gasped Janie, at last. "You were marvellous. But did you see her face when you said you were glad Jake had found his tongue at long last?"

Mrs Jarvis sank onto the sofa, wiping her eyes. "I thought she was going to burst with rage," she said.

Peter wrapped himself in the tablecloth and put a cushion on his head for a hat. "'If that is all he can use his tongue for,'" he mimicked, "'I hope he loses it for good!' Seriously, Jake," he added, pulling off the tablecloth, "you mustn't think Miss Dixon is typical of the people who go to our church. She's just an old hypocrite really, who only comes along to pull people to pieces. She's never approved of Mum and Dad being foster parents."

The postman had not shared in the helpless mirth with the rest of his family. He stood now by the window, looking rather miserable.

"We mustn't be too hard on her," he said quietly. "It was wrong of you, Jake, to use those words to anyone, but especially to a lady. All the same, she was very tactless, and I can quite understand the way you felt."

Jake went off to his room. The anticlimax of the mild rebuke irritated him. As he climbed the stairs, he heard the family collapse again with laughter. To cause this ridiculous family amusement was the last thing he intended to do.

After a few weeks with the Jarvises, the happiness that surrounded Jake began to unnerve him. He had never come across people like this before. They were noisy and untidy, but they never seemed to get angry with each other. And there was this ghastly God business. They couldn't even start a meal without chatting to Him as if they really thought He was sitting at the table with them. They didn't seem to mind about Jake's silence. They just talked to him all the time without ever actually asking direct questions, so he couldn't have the satisfaction of snubbing them.

He was also beginning to wonder if his first impression of the postman had been correct. Perhaps he was not such a fool after all. Sometimes he caught the little man looking at him. Jake had a spooky feeling that his private world of hatred was being penetrated by those gentle, kind eyes.

But it was Peter who bothered Jake the most. Why did someone tough like him, who was obviously good at sports and schoolwork, want to go fooling around with something like religion? Jake had never met anyone as happily uncomplicated as Peter, and he began to spend much of his time thinking of ways to ruffle his calm. Jake was a master of this art; he had been practising it for years. He played his radio very loudly when he knew Peter was doing his homework in the room below; he locked himself in the bathroom for ages when the older boy wanted a bath. Just before they left to catch the school bus, he would remove Peter's swimming trunks or running shorts from his school bag and the poor boy's pens, library books, and notebook paper kept disappearing and appearing again in a very odd manner. It was never anything very much, but added together the irritation must have been colossal. Day after day Jake waited for Peter to crack. He realised that Peter could beat him in any fight, but he longed for the satisfaction of seeing him roused. But after two weeks, Jake realised with disgust that his campaign was failing badly.

He must be as thick as his father, thought Jake bitterly. He just doesn't seem to notice. I'll have to do something really big, no matter what they do to me.

The opportunity came on the very next Saturday. Peter had been chosen to race for the area in a County Athletics Match. All the other Jarvises had gone along to watch. Football was Jake's first love; running around with no ball to chase seemed to him a farce.

"Now Jake," said Mrs Jarvis, "I've left you a nice cold lunch on the table. And if you get hungry again before we come back, you can raid the refrigerator. Are you quite sure you don't want to come, after all?" Jake scowled and turned his back on her. Two minutes later they were gone.

What fools to leave me here by myself! thought Jake. They must know about my record.

He went straight up to Peter's bedroom in search

of inspiration. But, simply because they had trusted him, he found it impossible to damage anything. Cross with himself, he wandered into the garden. Then he saw Peter's bicycle, leaning against the wall by the back door! A bicycle was a thing he had never had, and always wanted.

Let's have a spin for starters, he thought. The next minute he was sailing down the lane. The feelings that he experienced during the next half hour he remembered all his life. The thrill was indescribable. Jake only knew that to be alone in a world of speed, wind, and freedom was as satisfying to him as fire. As he rode back, the desire for a bicycle of his own filled his mind. Why should Peter have real parents of his own who loved him, a home he could never be kicked out of, and a bike to ride whenever he liked?

Jake enjoyed making that bonfire, in a grim kind of way. He had to use a great deal of the Jarvises' store of winter firewood to get it hot enough, because it is not easy to burn a bicycle. But he was not satisfied until he had put the bicycle pump into the flames as well.

Just the charred skeleton remained by the time he heard the Jarvises' old car spluttering into the garage. Peter's voice called, "I'm just nipping up to the village on my bike, Mum. I need some Coke." Then, a few minutes later, "Where *is* my bike, Mum? I'm sure I left it here by the back door."

Jake had made his bonfire at the end of the garden, in the right angle of the high stone wall. As Peter came toward him over the bumpy lawn, he wished he had not let himself be cornered.

"Where's my bike, Jake?" asked Peter quietly. He looked very big in his track suit, and the muscles of his arms were like molehills.

Have I gone too far? thought Jake as Peter caught sight of the twisted pieces of burnt bicycle. The older boy's face turned absolutely white and he took a quick step toward Jake.

Got him! thought Jake, suddenly triumphant. Whatever he does to me, it'll be worth it.

But Peter had stopped and his hands fell to his sides. "I'm going to tell you something," he said. "It's my birthday next week and Dad's saved up for a new racing bike for me. Only this afternoon, on our way home, I told him I wanted to give this bike to you. It's not my bicycle you've destroyed; it's your own." And seeing the stricken look in Jake's eyes, he turned and walked back into the house.

Alone by the smouldering fire, Jake wished intensely that Peter had hit him. He could then have hated him, instead of hating himself. As he looked down at the pieces of the burnt bike that might have been his own, he cursed himself for his stupidity.

3

Disaster for Streetfield

"It's the big game this week, Jake," said Peter one day, following the family's policy of talking to Jake as much as possible. "We've got the best village cricket team in the country. Next week our strongest rivals, Tidehurst, are coming for the biggest game of the season." His voice prattled on, with Jake only half listening. None of the Jarvises had ever once mentioned the burnt bike to him. Since that day he had given up his campaign of harassment toward Peter. Somehow it did not seem fun any more.

"We've got a super team," continued Peter. "Mike Turner opens for us, he plays for Cambridge, you know. Colonel White – he's the coach – saw me playing the other day and he said if I keep up the form I might be in the team next year."

Although Jake would never have admitted it to anyone, not even himself, he was beginning to enjoy Peter's company quite a lot. So that evening, he went with him to watch the Streetfield team practising.

They consisted mostly of the sons of the rich people who lived in the beautiful houses around the village square, or Green, as it was called. There were also a few muscly young farmers, as well as George, from the local garage.

Why can't they play a decent game like football? thought Jake.

"Never had a better chance of thrashin' that Tidehurst team," boomed the Colonel as the team sat on the steps of the cricket pavilion. "Half the county should be here to see fair play this weekend."

Peter was lying on his stomach in the soft grass worshipping the team from a respectful distance, while Jake sat and watched the evening shadows spreading across the velvet perfection of the field. The Streetfield cricket pitch, or playing area, was the village's pride and joy. Bored and irritated, Jake sneaked around the back of the pavilion and discovered the door of the groundsman's shed ajar.

Always curious, he slipped inside. There in the gloom, among mowers and brooms, he had his great idea. It was the sack marked "Weed Killer" that started his mind working.

"So half the county are coming to see fair play, are they?" he asked, smiling grimly. "They are going to see something more than usual this year."

Quickly he dragged the weed killer outside and hid it, together with a large watering can, behind some empty crates. After he had located an outside tap, he slipped home in the evening stillness. Later when the Colonel locked the door of the shed he didn't notice anything unusual. Whistling smugly, he swaggered home over the Green.

At first light next morning, Jake was up, dressed, and out. He judged correctly that no one in Streetfield would be around that early. He had learned a lot about weed killing from one of his foster fathers, who so hated weeds that he killed them with sadistic enjoyment, caring nothing for the flowers that died with them. Jake had often watched him mixing the white crystals in his watering can, so he knew just what to do now. Carrying the can to the middle of the famous grass-covered pitch, carefully and deliberately he went to work. He had to fill the watering can many times before he was satisfied. But, if Mr Percy of the Remedial Department could have seen him then, he would have realised that Jake could write extremely well.

Long before the milkman started his rounds, Jake was back home in bed. By the time a horrified groundsman had brought the Colonel from his elegant residence by the Green, it was too late to stop the damage.

"Don't tell a soul, whatever you do," breathed the

Colonel. "Just pray it won't show until after the weekend!"

The village was in a twitter of excitement that Saturday morning. George put up bunting all over the garage where he worked. Elegant ladies made extravagant cakes (for Streetfield Cricket Teas were famous), and the local newspaper sent over their chief reporter. But by the time the Tidehurst team arrived in a fleet of expensive cars the giggles and sniggers began. The faces of the Streetfield cricket team were purple with embarrassment as they read the incredibly rude word scrawled in scorched yellow grass right across their beloved pitch. To say they were put off their form was stating it mildly. Tidehurst beat them by ninety runs.

While the local policeman began his laborious inquiries, the newspaper reporter drove gleefully back to his office, planning such headlines as: *Village Shamed by Mystery Saboteur*. He wondered if his editor would let him quote the offending word. When the Tidehurst team had finally left, triumphant and hilarious, Mike Turner and some of the other younger members of the Streetfield team were left alone in the pavilion to lick their wounds of embarrassment.

"I could kill the pig who did that!" growled George, the man from the garage.

"Bet it was that red-faced kid the postman is fostering," drawled the Colonel's nephew.

"'Course it would be!" said George. "Why didn't we think of that before?"

"No one from *this* village would do such a ghastly thing," added Mike Turner. As they discussed the idea their indignation mounted.

"Nasty little vandal. Needs to be taught a lesson,"

they decided. As dusk fell, they set out to find Jake.

He had never been to a cricket match before, but he had really enjoyed that one! He was still chortling to himself as he sat on the top of a gate in the lane. They came out on him from the evening shadows like a pack of silent hounds, moving in for the kill. Jake smelt danger and his mouth went dry.

"Were you the vandal who made us the laughing-stock of the county?" demanded Mike. His hands on Jake's throat were like steel pincers. Jake knew they could never prove it but, as he looked at their faces, he also knew he could expect no mercy.

You're going to get the beating of your life, son, Jake thought, and there's nothing you can do about it!

The next few minutes were worse than he could have believed possible. They were five big fellows and they were very angry. Afterwards he could only remember an agonising confusion of kicking boots and crashing punches. His ears rang, his eyes were blinded by his own blood, and as he struggled to breath between kicks in his ribs and stomach, he wished they would give him one minute to be sick in peace.

Just when Jake really thought he was going to die, he heard Peter's familiar voice. "What do you think you're doing, you great thugs, mashing up a kid that size?"

The members of the cricket team were enjoying themselves for the first time that day. They had no intention of letting a fifteen-year-old like Peter stop their fun. So the Colonel's nephew jeered, "How do we know this one didn't help his little brother? We'd better give him a going over as well."

Jake heard a sickening thud and a cry of rage from

25

Peter. Just as the postman's old car chugged down the lane, Jake felt himself slipping into merciful darkness.

He knew no more until he opened his eyes to find himself lying on the couch in the Jarvises' cluttered sitting room. Peter was in the armchair holding a wet cloth to an ugly bruise on his cheek. He was still muttering furiously at the conduct of his ex-heroes.

Jake felt that he would never forget the way Mrs Jarvis was that evening. He vowed never to call her the Jelly Mountain again. She did not ask him any awkward questions or embarrass him by fussing too much. She just bathed, disinfected, and bandaged, as if Jake had been the most important person in the world to her. But it was the postman who helped him to force warm sweet tea between his cut and swollen lips. While Mr Jarvis held the cup he suddenly smiled and said, "We know you deserved all this, old son, but we're still terribly sorry it happened."

"Thank God you came along when you did, Dad," said Peter, lighting into a piece of his mother's chocolate cake. "They only hit me once, but wow! that made me mighty sorry for poor old Jake."

"We won't say anything about this to anyone," said Mr Jarvis firmly. "It might be a bit embarrassing with the police. And by the look of you tonight, Jake, I'd say you've been punished quite enough."

Later, when the postman and his wife had gone out to feed the rabbits and shut the chickens in for the night, Jake spoke for the first time in that house.

"Why were you on my side, back there?"

"I can't think," said Peter, laughing. "I'll never get into the team now."

"No, but why were you?" insisted Jake, finding himself desperate to know the answer.

"Oh well," replied Peter, lightly, "families have to stick together."

"Thanks, anyway," muttered Jake gruffly and closed his eyes.

It was a whole week before Jake was fit to go back to school. He had not been back there for more than three hours when he managed to throw the whole place into complete and utter confusion by sounding the fire alarm during the lunch period. No fire drill had ever before covered an emergency at that time of the day. The chaotic effect did a lot to restore Jake's bruised morale.

4

The Witch

For years Jake had made it his deliberate policy to hate everyone around him. But as the weeks went by, he found the Jarvises more and more difficult to hate. He had a panicky feeling that if he was not careful he would end up liking them instead. That would be such a terrible disaster that he felt he must get away from them as much as possible. That was easy enough during school hours, but what about all the rest of the time?

He discovered the woods, quite by accident, one

Sunday evening. Jake hated Sundays, but the evenings were the worst part. It was the same every week. By eight o'clock in the evening, the whole house was flooded with young people from all over the district. They came on bikes, on foot, in cars, or on motor bikes, and they took over the whole house. Singing with guitars, reading the Bible, and talking to God as if they knew him well. Jake could hear them even up in the attic, and he hated every one of them. The funny little postman seemed to be in charge, while his wife dished out cakes and coffee by the ton.

Jake would rather have died than go near them, but he always got a horrid feeling of being left out of the fun. On this particular Sunday he could stand it no longer. He banged out of the Scrap Heap, as he called the Jarvises' house, and stamped down the lane. Morosely he followed a footpath over the fields and suddenly found himself in the woods. The quietness and loneliness felt welcoming and he relaxed. No one was there among the great trees to stare at his birthmark, laugh at him for not being able to read, or to mock him for having no family of his own. He had somewhere to escape to now, and he went to the woods as often as he could during the week that followed. It was on Friday that he saw the rabbit. To a city-bred boy like Jake, the excitement of seeing a real wild rabbit was enormous and it gave him an idea.

On Saturdays, the Jarvises often went into town for a shopping trip and this time Jake went with them. Living in the country was certainly cheaper than city life, so Jake had quite a bit of money in the pocket of his jeans. With a cheerful, "Meet back here in an hour," the family dispersed in all directions.

Jake set off down High Street. Over the years he had perfected a way of getting sweets without having to pay for them. He would go into a shop jingling a few coins and, while taking a long time choosing how to spend them, he would fill his pockets with at least a pound's worth of his favourites. The ancient lady in the village shop at Streetfield was nearly blind, so he had not felt it a fair game to try this trick on her. But while he was in town, he seized his opportunity and "did" the three sweet shops on High Street before arriving at the sports shop he was looking for. There he bought a strong metal catapult and walked back to the car, well pleased with his morning.

The Jarvises sang hymns all the way home. It sounded terrible, but Jake had to hand it to them, they enjoyed life.

It rained hard all the rest of the day, so Jake had to wait until Sunday morning before going back to the woods with his new catapult stuck in his pocket.

He was a Wild Man now, and a Great Hunter. He would have swung from tree to tree if there had been any convenient vines around. He had a few unsuccessful shots at some birds, but it was really rabbits he was hunting. Then he saw the cat. She was a sleek black creature, like the pictures of a witch's cat on a broomstick. He never meant to kill her. He took aim without really thinking, using one of the round pebbles he had taken from Colonel White's driveway. He hit the cat between her eyes and she died instantly and without pain.

Jake stared down at her corpse as he fought a wave of nausea. She had been a beautiful creature and as he turned her over with his foot he realised she must have had kittens very recently. The pointless waste of the thing he had done hit him hard. Then, back into his mind rushed a terrible memory, a memory he had tried so hard to forget during the last three years. But still sometimes, when he least wanted to, his mind recalled that awful day and he heard again the terrible cries of the dog.

He had gone out to set fire to a scruffy piece of woodland in a park near the children's home. Earlier, he had borrowed a can of petrol from the house-parent's car and, with some matches, he was preparing for action when a large red setter came bounding up to him. He could not shoo it away and, in the end, had lost his temper. He threw petrol over the dog and lit a match. The effect was dramatic. The faster the terrified dog ran, the higher leaped the flames. In the confusion of screams and agonised cries that followed, Jake escaped. But for days he could not eat, and every time he closed his eyes to sleep, he saw the dog coming for him. Because of the devotion of his owner and the skill of the vet, the dog survived, but his coat never grew again. Every time Jake caught sight of the grotesque creature in the street he felt sick. Now this beautiful cat lay dead at his feet.

"What'll become of scum like you, Jake Jackson?" he muttered. "You're horrible right through."

The terrible depression that settled on him had to be shifted somehow, so he kicked the cat into the ditch. Chucking the catapult after it, he set off down the path in search of something to divert his mind.

He found it more quickly than he expected. Standing back from the path, surrounded by stinging nettles and the undergrowth, was what he took to be a deserted cottage. It had been part of an old mill two hundred years before when that part of Sussex had bustled with iron manufacturing. When the industry had died, most of the mill had fallen down, leaving only the miller's cottage to stand alone as the woods grew up around it. To Jake, in the mood he was in, it looked sinister. It occurred to him that this could be where the witch lived, whose cat he had just killed. He needed an adventure badly, so he pushed open the half-rotted gate and walked between the nettles to the front door.

"No one's lived here for years," he told himself firmly and peered through one of the front windows. Straight away he could see that he was wrong. The cottage was untidy, even worse than the Jarvises' house. But Jake could see that the furniture and ornaments were old and beautiful. It was then that he caught sight of the broomstick. It was leaning against the outside wall of the cottage, beyond the window where he stood.

"That proves there's a witch around here," he breathed, as a delicious thrill ran down his spine. He did not really believe in witches, but the whole idea fascinated him. He peered in all the windows, half hoping to catch sight of her, but no one seemed to be in. Perhaps the witch had gone to church with the Jarvises. No, witches were evil; they wouldn't like God any more than he did.

Then he had a really bad fright. As he looked through the dirty window, he saw in the dark corner of the gloomy sitting room a strange black shape, moving in an odd manner, near the floor. Jake would not have given it a second thought if he had not already scared himself by thoughts of witches.

He was half way to the gate when his curiosity checked his panic. He must know what that Thing was. Earlier he had noticed that the back kitchen window was partly open. It was not difficult for anyone with Jake's experience to be in the house in no time. The dirty kitchen smelt so dreadful that he had to hold his nose as he crept out into the little hallway and into the room where "It" was.

He needed all the courage he had to force himself across that dimly lit room. All at once he was standing looking down at a basket full of black kittens. The strange, moving shape that he had seen from the window was only all seven of them trying to climb out of their basket in a feeble search for their mother. They were only about a week old. Their eyes were not yet open and they looked so helpless! Since they were surely doomed to die, a lump rose in Jake's throat.

"I did for your ma, littl'uns," he whispered. "I'm sorry." He could feel the depression returning and he turned away from them. He must look at something else quickly. Something that was not dead or dying. On a small table, by the ash-filled fireplace, stood three little silver birds. They were perfect in every detail. Jake thought he had never seen anything as lovely, so he picked one up in each hand.

"I've got you!" rasped a voice from the doorway. Jake spun around and saw the witch, as a fresh wave of terror broke over him. She was extremely old and bent almost double. Straight white hair fell down either side of her thin face and she wore a long flannel nightgown. In her hand she held a pistol. Jake was confused. Witches muttered spells and waved broomsticks, but they never pointed guns. She looked at Jake with eyes that seemed red with anger and hatred.

"I won't shoot to kill," she said. "I'll just go for your knee, where it will hurt most. That will give me time to get up the path to the farmhouse and phone the police."

"Don't do that," said Jake quickly. "I haven't taken anything."

"Breaking and entering, that's a serious crime," she snapped, "and your fingerprints will be all over my birds. They'll send you to Borstal for that."

With his record, Jake knew she was right. He had always intended to ride away from Streetfield in a smart police car but, suddenly, that was the *last* thing he wanted to do.

"I know who you are," continued the rasping voice. "You're the postman's latest little convict."

"I'm not a convict," squeaked Jake indignantly.

"You will be when I've finished with you," cackled the witch.

Jake said no more. He was much too proud to whine and beg for mercy. The witch shuffled nearer to him and peered at his birthmark.

"Ugly little customer, aren't you?" she said unpleasantly. "But you look strong enough. See all those nettles and weeds out there?" She waved the pistol toward the window. Jake gulped and nodded. "There used to be a garden there once," she went on, "but this arthritis won't let me do anything about it now. If you come here two hours an evening, weekends as well, and clear that for me, I'll forget about this. But if you don't come, I'll go straight up to that phone."

"That's called blackmail," protested Jake.

"It's also called hard labour," cackled the old woman. "Which do you choose, my kind of justice or the police's?"

"Yours," muttered Jake, and swore rudely.

"I know a lot of worse words than those," said the

33

witch, as she marched Jake out through the smelly kitchen. Handing him a blunt sickle and a pair of rusty shears, she said, "Get started and don't expect a tea-break!"

The nettles stung his arms and legs, while the brambles tore his skin. The hot sun scorched him and the perspiration trickled down his neck. But every time he stopped work to straighten his back, the ugly old head shot out of the bedroom window and rained abuse and threats down upon him. As he crawled home at last, exhausted, bleeding, and stung, he was only thankful for one thing. That he had had the good sense to throw away the offending catapult.

5

Seven Black Kittens

The next week was a nightmare to Jake. He was so stiff from the hard work that he could hardly move in the mornings. He was so terrified the old woman would find out what he had done to her cat that he could not sleep at night. All day long he felt ill at school with fear of the very thought of having to go to that dreadful cottage again.

He laughed bitterly when he overheard Mrs Jarvis

say to her husband, "I hope Jake's all right, wandering about in the woods for so many hours every day."

"He'll come to no harm there," was the quiet reply. "Woods mend people."

He's got to be joking! thought Jake desperately. Of course, Jake didn't have to go back to that terrible place ever again. He had been in worse trouble than the witch could ever get him into. But something about this woman was so compelling and powerful that it forced him to do as she wanted.

It was Sunday again, at last. The heat pressed thickly down on him as he hacked at her weeds and brambles. He had barely started, but he already felt tired out. Suddenly the door creaked and the woman stood beckoning him from her doorstep. Jake slowly put down his pitchfork and apprehensively followed her into the cottage. In spite of the heat wave, he was ice-cold with fear when he realised she was taking him to where the kittens had been.

It will be all up with me, he thought, if she knows about the cat. But to his amazement, the kittens were all alive and looking very cheerful. Seven pairs of round blue eyes looked trustingly up at him from the basket.

"Their mother has gone off and deserted them, just as my mother did," spat the old woman. "Stupid cat! Gone off and found herself a smart young Tom, I expect, and left me holding the baby – all seven of them."

"Why aren't they dead, then?" asked Jake, as relief spread all over him.

"Why aren't they dead?" shouted the woman. "Because I feed them myself every two hours, day and night, and I'm completely exhausted. I even had to go on the bus into town to get this powdered kitten milk and these feeding droppers. All that effort, just to save their miserable hides. I ought to drown them."

"Oh, don't do that," begged Jake. "I'll help you feed them."

"In the mornings, before school?" she demanded.

"Yes," said Jake, wondering at himself. "I could be here about seven."

"Good!" she said. "I can have a rest and catch up with my reading. I've got all behind this week. You watch me this time and then you can do it yourself before you go home tonight."

Jake stood fascinated as she mixed the dried milk with warm boiled water. Then she put a glass tube into the mixture and squeezed the rubber bulb on one end, sucking a little of the milk up into the tube. Wrapping the first kitten in an old towel, she put the tube to its mouth. Instantly it began to suck vigorously and had swallowed three tubes full in no time.

"That's enough for you, you greedy thing," growled the woman, "or you'll burst your stomach."

She cursed and swore at each kitten as she fed it, but Jake noticed that her hands were gentle and kind.

"The stupid things think this hot water bottle is their mother," she explained as she put fresh hot water into it and, wrapping it in a rug, placed it back in the basket with the kittens.

"You have to keep them warm, even in summer," she told him. Then, to Jake's embarrassment, she picked up each in turn and rubbed their stomachs with a warm, damp piece of sponge.

"Human babies wet their nappies, but you have to

make kittens perform, just like the mother cat would." When each kitten had done all that it should, she replaced them on their hot water bottle and covered the basket with a blanket.

"You can get back to work, now," said the old woman. "Then you can do the next feed in two hours."

It was not as easy as it looked, especially with the woman breathing down his neck, cursing his clumsy fingers.

"Put the dropper in its mouth," she snarled. "It can't suck milk through its ear." And, "You'll strangle it, stupid boy, if you hold it like that." But by the time he had finished all seven, he was quite enjoying himself.

He certainly was not enjoying himself early next morning as he groped his way sleepily through the woods on an empty stomach. He could have kicked himself for offering to feed the kittens. But, as the days went by, he became more and more absorbed in them. He was soon giving them three and sometimes four of their daily feeds, as the old woman sat reading with her glasses perched on her purple nose.

Jake longed to know if anyone else was aware of the cottage and its ghastly owner, but because he did not speak to the Jarvises, he did not know how to find out.

So he was startled one day, on the way to the school bus, when Peter said, "If you go poking about in the woods much longer, you'll bump into Miss Potts. She's a terrible old woman. She lives in a tumbled-down cottage near the old iron mill. Have you seen her yet?" As Jake said nothing, Peter continued, "She's really horrible; no one goes near her unless they have to. She shouts dreadful things at

Dad when he has to go down there with her mail. She knows he's a Christian and she hates God, you see. I used to think she was a witch when I was small but Dad says she's not. She's just lonely and old. She seems to hate everyone, the way you do, Jake," he added with a grin. "You'll probably end up just like her."

Jake stopped dead in the middle of the lane. Would he really grow like Miss Potts, alone, feared, and shunned by everyone around him?

"Come on!" called Peter. "We'll miss the bus."

The idea worried Jake. He turned it over and over in his mind as he hacked at Miss Potts' undergrowth.

Why shouldn't I hate people? he thought defensively. They all hate me. They keep turning me out and kicking me around like a football. These Jarvises'll do just the same soon, when they get sick of me. At least I know where I am with this old woman. Her and me's got a lot that's the same.

The kittens grew at an incredible rate and, two weeks later, they were lapping porridge messily from a saucer and learning, quite successfully, to use their sand tray. Miss Potts carried their basket out into the evening sunshine so Jake could keep an eye on them as he worked. She let him burn up his rubbish at the end of every evening now, so, in spite of her abuse, he was almost beginning to enjoy himself.

One evening as he was leaning on his fork, watching the smoke and sparks rise into the darkening sky, Miss Potts hobbled up behind him with a string bag, full of books, in her hand.

"These kittens take up all my time," she complained. "I can't get into the library these days. You exchange these books before you come down here tomorrow. But don't bring me any silly detective stuff; I only like historical or travel books."

"Couldn't do that," said Jake flatly. "Can't read."

Miss Potts' thick eyebrows drew together in a frown. "What do you mean, you can't read?" she demanded. "You're twelve, aren't you?"

"I could if I tried," said Jake defensively. "But I don't want to, do I?"

Miss Potts pounced on him, like a cat on a mouse. "What do you mean, you don't want to read!" she shouted. "You're cutting yourself off from the greatest joy in life. People in books can't hurt you, so you don't have to hate them. I could teach you to read," she added, more quietly. "Fifty years ago I was a school teacher."

"Bet you were a horrible one," muttered Jake, wriggling out of her clutches.

"I was!" she said gleefully. "I made those nasty children work until they were ready to drop!"

"Well you can keep your reading, and your books," shouted Jake and, before she could hit him, he was off up the path to safety.

He was just settling down to sleep that night when he heard a knock on his bedroom door. Slipping out of bed he tugged open the door and saw the postman standing there.

"Mind if I come in and talk to you a minute, Jake?" he asked. Jake turned and sat down on the bed, a cold feeling spreading all over him.

He's come to break it to me, thought Jake. They're sending me back to the children's home.

The postman sat down on the end of the bed. "Your teacher, Mr Percy, asked me to go over and see him this afternoon," he began.

The fire alarm, thought Jake.

"He's a bit worried about you," Mr Jarvis

continued. "He thinks you're quite bright, but something seems to be stopping you from doing any work."

Jake sat on in stony silence.

"I'll make a deal with you," said Mr Jarvis, unexpectedly. "Colonel White's gardener broke his hip yesterday and I've been offered his job, until he's better. I can fit it in when I've finished my rounds. In three or four months, I reckon I could earn enough to buy you a really good bicycle. When Mr Percy tells me you are reading well and working hard, I'll give it to you."

A bike of his own, all shiny and new! Jake's heart leaped. But how did this odd little person know he wanted a bike that badly?

"Is the deal on?" asked the postman, and slowly, Jake shook the little man's hand.

Next evening, when Jake arrived at Miss Potts's house, she was sitting in the sun with her lap full of kittens. He said, "I changed my mind about reading. You can teach me, if you like."

"I changed mine, too," snapped the old woman. "Why should I waste my time on the likes of you?"

Jake was disappointed. He didn't want Mr Percy to teach him. That would have meant backing down.

"Go on," he wheedled. "I'd still do my full two hours' work and, if I could read, I'd exchange your books every week."

"Tiresome boy," grumbled Miss Potts. "Get on with your work!" But after the bonfire had burned out and they had watched the kittens lapping their supper, she pulled a small book from her shelf and said, "Come on then, let's get on with it."

It was an exhausting experience, being taught to read by someone like Miss Potts. But, because they understood each other, they made rapid progress.

School suddenly became a lot less boring and he even had to admit that maths, with the aid of a cassette player and a calculator, was quite good fun. Life was going well, until the fateful weekend of the Sunday school anniversary.

6

The Bomb in Church

"You coming to the sea with us on Saturday, Jake?" asked Janie Jarvis, her little round face red with excitement. "The whole Sunday school is going in a bus to Hastings. It's a lovely place."

"It won't only be kids," put in Peter. "The Sunday Evening Club is going as well."

The thought of himself on a Sunday school outing amused Jake greatly, but when Peter told him about the pier and amusement arcade, he decided to brave it.

It was good to have a day away from Miss Potts. As he bowled along in the bus, surrounded by cheerful people, he found he was enjoying himself. He disentangled himself from them all, however, when they arrived at the sea. He ambled away along the funny little streets. He soon discovered a marvellous little Joke and Trick Shop, tucked away in a dark alley. He had a wonderful hour there, poking about, and finally came away with a glass bottle marked "Extra Strong Stink Bomb". He even paid for it.

Better had, seeing I'm on the Sunday school trip, he thought. He had a vague idea of letting it off in school assembly. Just in case old Percy thinks I'm going soft with all this hard work I'm doing for him these days.

On the way home he found himself sitting next to a happily grubby Janie.

She's not a bad little kid, he thought as the bus lurched and rattled. Looks like her big brother really. Never stops talking either, same as him.

"It'll be ever so exciting tomorrow," she squeaked. "It's the Sunday school anniversary at our church and I'm in a play. We're doing Joshua and the walls of Jericho. I'm Rahab. Peter's playing the guitar for the songs the club is doing. Mum and Dad are running everything and we're even having the special speaker to lunch and tea. Mum's been cooking marvellous food all week." Jake listened to her endless prattle as an idea formed in his mind. What about a stink bomb in church? That would liven them all up a bit. But he would have to take it to church himself, and that wasn't so funny. Curiosity about what all these cheerful people did inside their little tin church had niggled him for weeks. So he was secretly glad to have a reason for going there.

It was unfortunate that when Jake arrived next morning the church was so full that the only empty seat was right next to Miss Dixon, the woman he had so offended on his first Sunday in Streetfield. She edged away from him as he sat down. But the face of the little postman, who was standing at the front, lit up at the sight of him.

Janie's play was pretty good, considering it was children's stuff, and the club was excellent. Although Jake would not let himself join in the singing afterwards, he had to admit he was enjoying himself thoroughly.

He had always thought church services were dismal and dull, but surely all these happy-looking people could not be afraid of God. The stink bomb was still in his hand, but the service was only halfway through when he decided not to use it.

Can't muck this up, he thought. It's too much fun.

It was the offering plate that caused disaster. His red-necked enemy, Miss Dixon, thrust the plate at him, as if she wished it had been a bayonet, and knocked the bottle out of his hand. In vain he dived under the chair for it, but the neck had broken and the evil fluid was already seeping out. As the visiting speaker began his talk, people started to sniff, discreetly at first, but soon handkerchiefs were coming out all over the church. People began to cough and sneeze. The Sunday school children in the front rows were the first to leave, giggling helplessly as they rushed for the doors. People were soon running in all directions as they gasped for fresh air. The special speaker was the last to leave the church, holding his notes, and pressing his handkerchief to his nose.

Under cover of the outcry, Jake slipped home and hid nervously in the shed, watching the rabbits chew their carrots.

"You let me down, Son," said a quiet voice behind him. Jake did not turn and the postman came and stood beside him.

"I can understand you having a lark. I was a boy myself once, but what you did today was a terrible thing. God is the most important person in the world to us. We owe him everything we have and you disgraced his house today and ruined the service he was enjoying." Jake looked around then, and he would rather have been beaten than see that look on the little man's face.

Dinner was a difficult meal. The visiting speaker did his best not to mention the service, but Mrs Jarvis was so upset that her carefully planned meal went very wrong. The Yorkshire puddings were flat, the gravy lumpy, and the custard burnt. When she finally disappeared to make a cup of tea, she didn't come back. On his way out, Jake saw her standing by the kitchen sink, crying.

Peter was waiting for him in the garden, and Jake had never seen him look so angry.

"You know what you've done, don't you?" Peter asked, and his voice grated. "That hypocrite of a woman you were sitting next to went and worked some of the elders up against Mum and Dad, after that service. They told Dad that if he couldn't control his own family better he ought to give up doing the Sunday school and the Club. He and Mum just live for all that, you know. And then the old beast got Mum in a corner and told her she was wicked to bring kids like you here, to corrupt all the youngsters in the district. It might have been funny if it hadn't upset Mum so badly. She's crying her eyes out in there now."

Jake went back into the rabbits' shed, cold with misery. He had spent hours, when he first came, thinking of ways to hurt these people. Now he had managed it perfectly. But it had brought him no enjoyment. Every single prank that he had played in this village had misfired on him badly.

The speaker left hastily in his car, not waiting for the marvellous tea Mrs Jarvis planned for him. When Jake walked through the house to change for Miss Potts, he saw his foster parents sitting together on the couch. The postman had his arms around his enormous wife, who held a handkerchief to her eyes. Jake remembered how kind she had been to him as he lay on that same couch, after the Tidehurst cricket match.

Suddenly Jake did something he had never, ever done before in his life. He crossed the room and, standing before them, said gruffly, "I'm sorry. I'll never do anything like that again."

Not waiting to change his clothes, he made for the woods.

"He spoke to us!" exclaimed Mrs Jarvis, her tears gone for good.

"That's the first time ever!" said her husband.

"You could see he really meant it, as well. It makes it all worthwhile, whatever anyone says about us."

When Jake returned, rather nervously from work, he discovered that being sorry and saying so had quite restored the gaiety of the household. Peter even said, as they sat down to the special tea, "How nice to be able to eat all this and not have to be polite to a visitor." Mrs Jarvis pretended to scold him, but soon they were all laughing. Jake found himself helping to wash up like one of the family.

The rumblings from the village continued, however, and on Monday evening the Jarvises had a long visit from their minister. Jake was up in his room, actually doing some homework, and he heard the postman say, quite loudly and sharply for him, "Shouldn't we be praying for him, instead of criticising?" The following day, when Janie came home from school, she found her mother in tears again, after a visit from Miss Dixon.

"She wants us to send Jake back to the children's home," she told her daughter with an indignant sniff.

The television was on so loudly that neither of them heard Jake come quietly into the empty kitchen. He was just in time to hear Janie say, "But why do we have to have a boy like Jake in our family if it makes everyone cross with us?" Tensely, Jake waited for the answer.

"Because God sent him to us, my dear," said Mrs Jarvis. "He loves Jake very much, you see."

"But God surely wouldn't care about a boy like Jake," protested Janie.

"That's just the wonderful thing," was the reply. "He loves him just as much as he loves you, or Peter, and really cares about what happens to him."

Jake slipped quietly out of the back door again and made for his beloved woods.

He had always wondered why this mad family had offered him a home, and why, in spite of his scowls and deliberate silence, they had not sent him away long ago. He supposed it was because "being good with difficult cases" made them feel big.

But here was Mrs Jarvis saying it was because God had sent him to them, because he cared about him. No one had ever cared before. Not his Irish mother, his social worker, or any of the innumerable people who had looked after him. Was God different from all of them? Was Mrs Jarvis right? And what about the woman in the children's home who said God hated and punished wicked people?

His head was so full of all these questions that during their reading lesson that evening he asked

Miss Potts, "Could God love people like you and me?"

The old lady looked as if she had seen a poisonous snake. "That dratted postman's been getting at you!" she snarled. "You can take *that* for asking such silly questions."

Rubbing his tingling ear, Jake continued with his lesson. But the idea that God could love him filled his mind for days.

7

Over the Cliff

It was the first day of the summer holidays. The nicest day of the whole year.

"I wish we were going on holiday, though," said Janie. "Everyone else is."

"We just can't afford it this year, my love," said Mr Jarvis. "But I tell you what we'll do. I've got the day off tomorrow. Why don't all three of you choose a friend and we'll squeeze into the car and go off for a day out?"

Janie squealed with delight. "I'll take Ann," she said and rushed off to arrange it.

Jake felt embarrassed. He had no friend he could ask. Suddenly he caught Peter's eye and sensed the older boy understood.

"I'll take Jake as my friend, if he'll have me," said Peter, grinning. "It'll make more room in the car." Jake felt relieved and resentful all at the same time.

They left very early in the morning. Janie and her gappy-toothed Ann giggled all the way. But the long journey was worth it when they got there. In the country park were miles of woods and hills, with great white cliffs, looking out across the sea to France.

Mr and Mrs Jarvis and the little girls were content to stay on the pebbly beach. But Peter and Jake explored for miles around and had enormous fun. Doing things with someone else was much more exciting than being alone. Jake wished the day would last forever. After their picnic lunch, the boys went off to the shop by the car park to spend their money. Jake suddenly felt so grateful to Peter for everything that day that he wanted to do something for him. He waited until Peter was absorbed by the guide books and pamphlets, and no one else was looking. Then Jake filled his pockets until they bulged with sweets from the shelves.

"Let's walk up the river now," said Peter, when they were outside again. "We might spot some herons."

"I've got something for you," said Jake proudly. With a flourish, he spread out the sweets on one of the picnic tables under the trees.

"Thanks!" said Peter licking his lips. "You must be wealthy to afford all that."

"Oh, I didn't buy it," said Jake, laughing.

Peter frowned. "You mean you pinched them?"

"'Course," said Jake impatiently. "Everyone does. They ought to watch their stuff more carefully if they don't want it nicked." Peter for once said nothing. He didn't seem to know what to say.

Suddenly a shadow fell across the picnic bench and they both looked up guiltily. It was the postman.

It would be, thought Jake bitterly as he tried to cover the sweets with his jacket.

"Did you pay for all that, Jake?"

"'Course I did!"

"Jake," said the postman quietly. Anger boiled up inside the boy. This ridiculous little man could read people's thoughts.

"Well, everyone does it," he repeated hotly.

"You are a member of my family now, and so you will not steal," said Mr Jarvis in a tone Jake had never heard him use before. "We're going to the shop to return it and you're going to apologise."

"You've got to be joking!" said Jake defiantly.

"I'm not joking," said Mr Jarvis firmly.

Who does he think he is? thought Jake furiously. He's no bigger than I am; he can't make me do anything I don't want to do.

But those compelling eyes continued to bore two holes through Jake. He found himself gathering up the sweets and following the little man back into the shop. Three months before, he would not have believed it was possible.

The next few minutes were incredibly embarrassing for everyone concerned. The manager of the shop said they would not prosecute because the sweets had been returned, but Jake wished he could smash the man's face in. When it was all over, he pushed his way rudely out of the shop. He felt angry and ashamed. It had been so wonderful, having Peter as a friend all day, but now everything was ruined. Peter would never like him again. He stormed off up the cliff path.

"Let him go, Pete," said the postman gently. "He's upset. He'll come around if we leave him alone."

But Jake yearned for Peter to follow him. They'll call Fat Toad Lewis tonight, he thought miserably. They won't keep me any longer now.

He did not mean to jump over the cliff. He would never really have dared to anyway. He just wanted to hurt the Jarvises somehow, and frighten them. He stood at the edge watching the sea churning and frothing far below him. He could see the rest of the family on the beach, away down on his right.

They'll come and look for me sometime, he thought bitterly. Sure enough, when the sun began to dip towards the sea, he saw the postman and his son begin to climb the path toward him.

I'll wait until they are nearly here, then I'll pretend I'm going to go jump over, he thought. That'll make them sorry.

But the idea went badly wrong. As he stood on the very edge, he suddenly lost his balance. Scrambling wildly at the rocks, he began to fall. Fortunately the upper part of the cliff was not completely sheer at that point. He had not fallen more than twenty yards when he hit a small ledge where seagulls nested. He rolled off it, but not before he had instinctively grabbed a small bush which struggled to survive there. Its roots were so short that it was a miracle it supported his weight at all. As he hung below the ledge, he felt it giving away. Two faces appeared above him, whiter than the chalk of the cliff.

"I can't hold on," Jake croaked in terror.

"Go and get help, Pete," said the postman. "I'm going down to pull him onto that ledge."

"You can't do that, Dad," protested Peter.

"You'll kill yourself!"

"He won't be able to hold on more than a minute or two," replied his father. "I can't just sit here and watch him fall." Without another word, Peter was off towards the Field Centre. If he had been at an athletics match he would have broken quite a few records.

"Hold tight, son. I'm coming!" called the man Jake had once despised.

Without ropes or climbing experience it was an incredibly dangerous thing to attempt. Jake realised the postman was risking his life, but he could feel the cramp beginning in his arm muscles. Every time Jake moved, the stupid little bush creaked ominously. Far below, the sea washed over the rocks, waiting for both of them.

Bit by bit, the postman edged his way down, spread-eagled against the rock, chatting calmly to Jake all the time, for all the world as if he had been shaving in the bathroom at home.

Suddenly and miraculously, he was on the ledge and bracing his back against the cliff face. He had Jake up beside him just before the panic-stricken boy was sick.

"I ought to thump you," he said with a grin, when Jake's teeth had stopped chattering. "But I reckon we'd both be in the sea if I did!" Jake gazed at him in wonder. There he sat laughing and joking as if he had been on the beach, eating ice cream. He had often wondered what all those big fellows who came every Sunday evening could see in this ridiculous little man. He knew now.

He's brave as a lion! thought Jake, closing his eyes tightly.

The rescue party did not take long to reach them,

thanks to Peter's wonderful sprint. They were soon walking shakily down the path to the beach.

"Don't tell your mother, whatever you do," warned the postman. But they were all quite drunk with relief and they cracked jokes and laughed hilariously all the way home.

"You three have been up to something," said Mrs Jarvis suspiciously. "You're worse than the girls. Three big men like you ought to be ashamed of giggling like that."

"Good night, son," said the postman later. Something about the way he put his hand on Jake's shoulder made the boy feel ill with longing to be a real part of this extraordinary family.

8

The Tragic Accident

It was during the summer holidays that the Jarvises' dog was due to have her puppies. She was the most valuable thing they possessed and they all adored her. She had been given to Mrs Jarvis as a small pup by the mother of a child she looked after during the day. This woman bred and showed Shelties all over the country.

"Two of the pups will have to be given back to her," Janie explained to Jake. "But the others will be worth a lot of money. Dad says if everything goes well, we could all afford to go on a real holiday next year. Let's keep our fingers crossed so she has a big litter." The dog, who was called Happy, loved Janie best of all and even met the little girl when she came home from school. Jake, however, could never bring himself to touch a dog since the affair of the red setter.

It was impossible to keep his visits to Miss Potts a secret. Now the holidays meant that Peter's mind was not taken up with homework and athletics. One day, as Jake was grubbing out bramble roots, Peter came down the path through the trees and stood gazing over the garden gate.

"I must say you've done marvels here!" he said admiringly. "The whole place looks quite neat. Imagine you going off and getting yourself a job on the side." Dropping his voice, he added, "They say the old girl's got masses of money stashed away in there. Does she pay you well?"

"Well enough," answered Jake. "But she'll come out and clout me, if I keep talking to you all day."

"All right," said Peter cheerfully. "But when you're finished here I'll take you up to the Rec. The football season will be on us next term and I could give you some coaching."

Jake felt quite light-headed with happiness as he watched Peter walking away, with Happy waddling at his heels. Could this mean that Peter still wanted to be his friend?

That evening Peter had quite a shock. After half an hour up at the Recreation Ground, he realised that there was nothing about football that he could ever teach Jake. Red in the face, he flung himself down on the ground to rest.

"I've got to hand it to you, Jake," he panted. "You know how to control that ball. Why didn't you tell me you could play like that? You'll knock spots off anyone else in your class and probably the class or two above!"

They spent hours together up at the Rec after that, and soon Jake had won Peter's complete admiration. It did not seem to matter which way he was facing, he could still turn and hit the ball into the middle of the goal with either foot. But when any of the other village boys came up for a game, Jake would toss the ball to Peter and amble away, saying, "I'm fed up now, Pete. See you."

It was most inconvenient of Happy to start having her puppies right in the middle of Club, on a Sunday evening. Jake had started joining in now and was even learning some of the songs. He went to church, as well, telling himself it was just to irritate the old buzzard who was gunning for him. But deep down he knew it was because he wanted to discover more about God.

They were in the middle of a fascinating discussion on the ways God talks to people, when Janie's voice called from upstairs.

"Quick, something's happening up here!" Considering how Happy loved the little girl, it was not surprising that she should have chosen to have her puppies on the little girl's bed. The puppies arrived at regular intervals during the night, and no one had any sleep, even though she managed the whole thing herself, very efficiently. At dawn there were five little Sheltie pups cuddling up to Happy, sucking vigorously.

Everyone crawled off to bed for a couple of hours of sleep, except Janie, who had to have a sleeping bag on the floor beside her new charges.

All went wonderfully for the first eight days. The puppies were healthy and Janie was ecstatic. Then a terrible thing happened. It was Monday afternoon and Jake was at loose ends. He had been to Miss Potts's house in the morning. Now he had nothing to do until Peter came back from the dentist, where he had gone with his mother and Janie. Jake ambled up to the village and over the Green to see how the damaged pitch was coming on. At the far end of the Green he noticed Mr Jarvis, cutting the hedge in Colonel White's garden. As he drew nearer, he noticed how tired and hot the little man looked. Jake knew only too well what hard work it was toiling in someone else's garden.

"I'll sweep up the trimmings for you," he offered, as he pushed open the wrought iron gate and entered the beautiful garden.

"Thanks," said the postman pleasantly. They worked in happy silence, each content with his own thoughts. The postman was an easy man to be with, and Jake always found his company very soothing.

Suddenly the dreamy peace of the afternoon was shattered. The French doors burst open and the squat figure of the Colonel positively stamped over the lawn toward them.

"Jarvis!" he shouted. "Get that boy out of my garden! I know he ruined our pitch. If you ever bring him here again, I'll give you the sack. Understand?"

"Better push off home, Jake," said the little man mildly, when the Colonel had stumped off to his garage. "I couldn't get you that bike if I lost this job."

"I hate him," growled Jake through clenched teeth.

"You shouldn't," said the postman pleasantly. "God loves him, same as he loves Miss Potts."

"Bah!" said Jake and slammed the iron gate.

He was nearly home when he heard a car speeding down the lane behind him. It was the Colonel. He still seemed in a bad temper because his face was purple and he was driving far too fast. Jake did not see Happy soon enough. It was the first time she had left her puppies to take a walk in the lane. She was really looking for Janie.

"Look out, Happy!" shouted Jake in horror, but it was too late. The Colonel's car hit her with deadly force.

"Stupid dog!" shouted the Colonel, skidding to a halt. "Why couldn't you have kept it under control?" As he reared off up the lane, Jake stood looking down at Happy. She was obviously dead, but he did not want Janie to see her like this. Carefully he carried her into the garden and went to the shed to look for a spade. It was hard work digging in the dry ground, but Happy was safely buried when he heard the car arrive home.

I can't tell the poor kid, thought Jake, his mouth suddenly turning dry. Then to his relief he saw Mr Jarvis coming in through the gate.

"Make us a cup of tea, Mum," called Mr Jarvis, mopping his red face. "I'm just about all in."

"Could I talk to you, before you go in?" asked Jake.

"What's up, son?" he asked kindly when he saw Jake's face. Jake took him to the grave and told him what had happened. Then, together they went into the house to break the news to the family.

Janie sat very still on the couch, trying hard not to cry. "Anyway," she said, "I've still got the puppies." Then she stopped and her little face turned very white. "Can they live without Happy to feed them?"

"I'm afraid not, love," said her mother gently. "Daddy better put them out of their misery quickly. We wouldn't want them to suffer, would we?"

"Don't do that," said Jake quickly.

"We couldn't rear them," said the postman. "We don't know anything about puppies."

"I do," said Jake firmly. "Please give me a chance."

"Let him try," pleaded Janie desperately.

Through the woods dashed Jake, faster than he ever had before. Miss Potts, in the middle of her afternoon sleep, was far from pleased to see him.

"The dog's been killed," panted Jake. "Do you think puppies can be reared like kittens?"

"How should I know! I hate dogs," she snapped.

"Well, would you lend me the droppers and that bit of leftover milk powder, just until I can get into town tomorrow for more?"

"Take anything you like," retorted the old woman, "if it means I can have some peace."

It was a strange feeling for Jake to be in charge of a situation. He found a suitable-sized box and showed Mrs Jarvis exactly the right temperature for the hot water bottle. He sent Janie to fetch her doll's blanket and showed Peter how to sterilise the feeding equipment. Carefully he mixed the feed and showed Janie how to use the droppers.

"Don't give them more than three tubes full until they get bigger," he said knowledgably, "or you'll bust them." When he finished up by sponging their tail ends, the family's admiration was complete.

"You're a wonder, you are, Jake," said Mrs Jarvis

as they put the box in the kitchen to keep warm.

"We'll feed them every two hours, in the night as well," said Jake. "We can take turns."

The puppies seemed quite contented and everyone was too busy to think much about Happy. But that evening Jake found Janie crying beside the box of puppies, with Happy's lead in her hand.

"You've still got the puppies," he said gruffly. And then, to his embarrassment, he found her hand in his.

"Oh Jake," she said, "if it hadn't been for you I couldn't have stayed alive through today." Jake shook her hand away, but he felt warm all over.

Those summer holidays were just too busy to leave Jake time to get into any trouble. He went to Miss Potts's house each morning. When there was nothing more to do in the garden, she set him to repaint her window frames and doors. When he tentatively suggested that he had "done his time," she cuffed him and said, "You're paying for your reading lessons now, boy, so get on with it." Because he had a sneaking liking for the old girl, he made no more objections.

His saving of the puppies had won for him Janie's complete devotion. Under Jake's instruction she brought them up most efficiently. She and Jake had their hands full keeping the puppies from chewing the Jarvises' house to pieces. Janie hadn't the time to grieve for Happy long.

When Peter and Jake were not kicking a football up at the Rec, they went fishing in the local river, or swimming at the pool in town. Theirs was a strange relationship, with Jake almost completely silent and Peter talking continuously. But the summer days were never dull for either of them.

Jake might have been happy if it had not been for the nagging feeling at the back of his mind that he must not get too close to the Jarvises.

It'll hurt more when they send me back, he thought.

9

The Parker War

One day in early September, when Jake was reading to Miss Potts, she suddenly said, "That teacher of yours is going to be quite pleased with you when you get back to school." Jake had to admit he was rather looking forward to the beginning of the term. But a week later Jake's life had changed drastically. When he got back to school, he found that Mr Percy had been transferred to another department. A bulging-necked new teacher, called Parker, had taken over Noddy Land, as the Remedial Department was nicknamed.

He began the first morning by locking away all the calculators and cassette lessons, and pulling piles of shabby textbooks from another cupboard.

"Listen to me, you horrible lot!" he roared. "I'm going to ram the three Rs down your throats the good old-fashioned way, and you'll leave here literate or dead! Do you hear?" Jake hated him on sight and, putting his feet up on his desk, lit a cigarette. Mr Parker's great bulk loomed over him at once.

"I've read your records, Jackson," he said, his red-rimmed eyes glaring down on Jake. "I'm telling you now, I'm going to make your life not worth living."

All right, thought Jake, as he watched his cigarette being extinguished beneath Mr Parker's heel, if that's the way you want it, two can play at that game.

From that day on, there was open war between them. Not one stroke of work did Mr Parker get out of Jake. And Jake was able to prevent everyone else in the department from working, too. Sometimes, however, when the school bus stopped in the village, Jake could see the postman sweeping the autumn leaves from Colonel White's lawns. He felt sick with despair when he thought about his bicycle.

Things were almost as bad for Jake in the PE department at school. He knew he could beat any boy in his class on the football field but, somehow, he could not give the muscly giant, Mr Ranson, the satisfaction of seeing him do anything well. In vain did the PE teacher shout at him.

"Why are you such an idiot, Jake?" asked Peter one day. He had found Jake hanging around in the corridor when he ought to have been on the football field. "You could be playing for England, one day, if you weren't such a fool."

As the weeks went on, Mr Parker grew more and more infuriated.

"That boy Jackson ought to be in a special school," he grumbled one day in the staff room. "He's quite uneducable."

"Oh, I don't know," said Mr Percy, pouring

himself more coffee. "He worked very well for me, at the end of last year."

"You young teachers are all the same," boomed Mr Parker, his neck turning purple. "Too soft! That's what's wrong with education these days! I'm going to have a word with the Headmaster right now about getting him transferred." As he slammed out of the room, Mr Percy looked worried.

It was the next day, when Jake was whiling away his PE period in the corridor, that he hit on a way of passing the time. Finding some white cards, he wrote, *Out of Order* on each one and then quickly fastened them to every toilet door in the school. The confusion was complete and Jake was happy to own up, just to see Mr Parker's face.

"You're coming to the Headmaster with me, my lad," he roared, dragging Jake through the hall.

Not only did the Headmaster have a sense of humour, but he was also becoming irritated by Mr Parker. He said, when they arrived in his office, "Yesterday, Parker, you told me this boy was educationally subnormal. If that is so, how did he write *Out of Order* so clearly and so many times? All the same, Jackson, on Mr Parker's advice, I have made arrangements for you to see a school psychologist later this term." And when he had rather half-heartedly scolded Jake, he waved them both away.

Outside the office door, Mr Parker said, "Listen here, Jackson, I'm going to see that you are sent away to a boarding school for maladjusted children if it's the last thing I do. It will give me great pleasure to get you out of my hair."

Jake looked up at his bald head and laughed rudely, but inside he was not laughing at all. How could he live if he had to leave Streetfield, the Jarvises, Miss Potts, the woods, and the puppies? He locked himself in the coat room and prayed for the first time in his life. "God, if you really do love me, don't let them do that to me."

"What's the matter with you tonight, Boy?" complained Miss Potts. Now that the dark evening had closed in, they were sitting by a huge fire of logs that Jake had chopped earlier. They were having their reading lesson, but the words in the book sounded like gibberish.

"I don't know if I want to come here and read any more," said Jake listlessly.

"What do you mean?" snapped the old woman.

"There's not much point really," said Jake. "They're going to send me away to a boarding school for backward children."

Miss Potts let fall a string of oaths and then asked why.

"Well," explained Jake, "I've got this great beast of a teacher this term and he hates my guts, like I hate his. Because I won't do any work for him, he's making me see a psycho-something to have me put away."

"And you're so stupid, you deserve it," shrilled Miss Potts.

"What d'you mean?" demanded Jake indignantly. "I can read all right now, can't I?"

"'Course you can," she snapped back. "You're just playing into this bully's hands by refusing to work. You could make him look a terrible fool if you showed him what you could do. When that psychologist fella looks at your exercise books he'll give your teacher 'what for,' for wasting his time. That's the way to get even with him," she finished, stabbing the fire viciously with the poker.

The idea appealed to Jake as he thought it over during the night.

Next day, at school, Mr Parker had a surprise. When he handed out the English textbooks, Jake took his and began to work at once. All day long Jake remained with his head down, getting through an unbelievable amount of work. By the end of the day Mr Parker was astounded and not a little put out.

The battle between them raged on, with Mr Parker taking a delight in setting work for Jake that he thought was too difficult, and Jake working away at it until his brain ached, but his answers came out right. He was given hours of homework which he did in Miss Potts's cottage, with her gleeful help.

The Headmaster had informed Mr Jarvis that Jake would be seeing the school's psychologist on December fourth. He said nothing to Jake, but as the little man was delivering the morning's letters, he sent up a prayer for him as he watched the school bus disappear down the road.

The psychologist was a jolly little fat man with twinkly eyes. Jake didn't feel too frightened of him when he was ushered in to see him at eleven o'clock that day.

"Sit down," said the man pleasantly. He began to rustle through the many files, letters, exercise books, and record cards that all carried Jake's name.

"Mr Parker seems a bit worried about you," he said at length. "Why's that, do you think?"

"Mr Parker's an old pig, sir," said Jake quietly. During the ten minutes that the psychologist had spent with Mr Parker, earlier that morning, he had come to much the same conclusion.

"You got on all right with Mr Percy, last term,

though, didn't you? I have a report here from him which says you began to work wonderfully all of a sudden. Why was that?"

Jake was almost beginning to like the man by this time, so he said, "My foster dad promised me a bike, you see."

The psychologist grinned at him over the desk. Suddenly the last of Jake's nervousness left him and he was able to do, quite superbly, the various tests which followed. When the jolly little man had looked with interest through some of Jake's more recent work, he whistled softly, shook Jake's hand, and sent him back to his class.

"Well, what do you make of him?" asked the Headmaster, as the two men drank coffee together, later that day. The psychologist grinned at him. "He really has no business in your Remedial Department," he said "His IQ is at least a hundred and fifteen and his reading age is fifteen plus. I wouldn't be surprised to see him leaving here with top marks. *But*," he added, setting his cup down with a sudden angry snap, "if I were you, I wouldn't have Parker here, even as a janitor!"

The postman had to deliver the brown envelope to himself, but he could not work up nerve to open it until he and his wife were alone together at midday.

"It's from the school," he said fingering it nervously. "I recognise the envelope. It will be about Jake going to that maladjusted school. The psychologist was seeing him about it on Monday."

"We can't let them send him away, can we?" asked Mrs Jarvis miserably.

"He's caused us more headaches than any of the others we've had," said her husband with a sigh. "But I'd miss him dreadfully if he wasn't here any more." He read the letter through in silence and then poked it over the table to his wife. It would have done Jake good if he could have seen the look of relief which spread across her face.

That day, when the school bus stopped by the village Green, Mr Jarvis was not working in Colonel White's garden. His battered old car was parked near the bus stop and, as Jake and Peter climbed out, he wound down his window and shouted, "Hop in, boys, we're going back into town." He would answer no questions and, half an hour later, they were in the best bicycle shop in the district. Ten minutes after that, Jake was the very proud owner of a magnificent sports bike with a lightweight frame and double horn.

10

The Football Game

During the next few weekends, as Jake raced Peter around the frosty lanes, their bikes whistling beneath them, he often thought about that desperate prayer he had uttered at school. It had been answered so satisfactorily that one Sunday night, during Club, he even got as far as whispering, "thank you," under his breath. A young man from a church in town had come to speak to them that evening. He stuttered and stumbled his way through his talk, but when he used the word *adoption* Jake sat up very straight.

"God loves us so much," stammered the speaker, "that he wants to adopt each of us as his own children. Being an adopted child is even more wonderful than being born into a family, because someone has to love you very much and choose you personally to adopt you. I, myself, was adopted at the age of six and it made all the difference to me. I felt I belonged to my new family forever, safe somehow, and very specially loved." Jake listened to no more. For as far back as he could remember, he had longed to be adopted. But Mr Lewis had told him firmly once that he was quite unsuitable. Would God think he was unsuitable as well? When the young man had come to a stumbling halt and everyone was drinking coffee and eating Mrs Jarvis's homemade biscuits, Jake cornered the speaker and asked him right out, "how can I get adopted by God?"

"You just ask," was the simple reply.

"But I've been in a lot of trouble, see," explained Jake. "How would God feel about someone with my record?"

"Well, when any of us want to be adopted by God," the young man answered, "we have to tell him first about the bad things we've done, and if we're really sorry he forgets them completely."

Like the Jarvises and the stink bomb, thought Jake as a great big lump gathered in his throat.

"You mean that's all I have to do and God'll have me?" he asked.

"That's right," said the nervous speaker with a smile. "You could do it now, if you like."

"Yes do, Jake," urged Peter, who was standing close by. "I did it last year."

"Oh, no!" said Jake quickly. "I don't know if it's for me yet, do I? I'm not going to make a fool of myself and then find God turns me down."

Leaving the young man looking rather puzzled, Jake went up to his room.

"How do I know you're not mucking about, God?" he prayed. "Surely you don't love someone like me." Once he'd thought religion was no good, but now it all seemed to matter more than anything else in life. He turned off the light and lay for hours thinking deeply.

When he woke in the morning, everything was clear in his mind. He had to have some definite sign before he could be sure all this wasn't made up by the Jarvises and their friends.

"If they don't chuck me out of here," he prayed as he pulled on his clothes, "then I'll know it's all for real and I'll come to you with all them bad things, what I done, and I'll say sorry and ask you to adopt me." It was as simple as that to Jake. He waited calmly to see what would happen.

The joy of being out of Noddy Land for good and in the main hectic life of the school was greater than Jake could have believed possible. But the problem of Mr Ranson and PE was still unresolved.

"Peter Jarvis tells me you're a real superstar when you're out of school," bawled the poor frustrated teacher. "So why don't you bring your boots and kit and stop being so pig-headed?" Jake would have liked to do just that, but it had become such an issue by then that he did not know how to back down without feeling like a fool.

The game with Hurley School was set for mid-January and Peter was naturally goalkeeper for the fifteens-and-under team. He told the family about the strategy at breakfast on the day of the game. "Those Hurley players think they're all bionic."

"Will you win, do you think?" asked the postman, who was off duty that day.

"Well," said Peter with his mouth full, "they always beat us, but we're playing a new boy called Stephen Davson now and Mr Ranson thinks we might have a chance this time."

The postman was taking Peter and another boy from Streetfield direct to Hurley. As there was a spare seat in the car, Jake went too. When the team arrived in their football uniforms on the well-kept playing fields of Hurley, they were greeted by a tense Mr Ranson. It mattered to him greatly that they beat this supercilious team, for he had a personal vendetta against their PE teacher. His reputation as a coach was at stake over this game.

"Where's Davson?" he asked tensely. Someone said he hadn't arrived yet, so Mr Ranson began his pregame pep talk with many an anxious glance at his watch. Suddenly the Headmaster of Hurley came hurrying over the frosty field.

"There's been a phone call," he puffed. "I'm afraid one of your team's had a car accident on the way here. He and his father are in Hurley Hospital."

"Why did it have to be Davson?" moaned Mr Ranson. "He was our only hope."

Hurley's irritating PE teacher strolled over and said, "Can't you find a substitute? We really ought to make a start; my boys are getting cold."

Mr Ranson ran a distracted eye over the supporters, but they were either over fifteen or without boots, and neither of the reserves had turned up.

"Your boots are in the back of Dad's car," said Peter, grabbing Jake's arm. "You left them there when Dad gave us a lift back from the Rec last Saturday."

"I'm not playing in the game," said Jake firmly.

"Please," said Peter. "I know you can do it." He looked so desperate that Jake relented.

"Him!" said Mr Ranson, when Peter said Jake was willing to play.

"It would be better than going in a man short," pointed out Peter.

Mr Ranson knew he was in for a humiliating morning anyway, so with a shrug he went off to bundle Jake into a uniform.

Back on the field again, Jake was greeted by the usual snickers and jeers from the Hurley team, but it was the "black and white and red all over" joke that finally put him in the right mood for the game. When the referee blew for the kick-off, he was down the field like a mad thing.

Mr Ranson never forgot that game. Standing by his enemy on the sideline, he first noticed Jake as he collected the ball in mid-field, slipped past three defenders, pushed the ball onto his left foot, and hammered it into the back of the net, leaving the astonished goalkeeper gaping. His bored resignation changed to mounting excitement and by the time Jake scored again, he was almost jumping up and down.

"That little reserve of yours with the birthmark's got some talent," conceded his enemy grudgingly. "Is he really younger than the rest or just small for his age?"

"Only just thirteen," said Mr Ranson. "Of course, I've given him a lot of coaching," he added, feeling rather ashamed of himself. Peter was also playing the game of his life as goalkeeper. The Hurley boys were beginning to look a bit sick when, at half time, they still had not scored.

During the half time, their coach called them around him. Whatever he said to them, Mr Ranson wished he had heard it, because they came out onto the field again like a pack of starving wolves. Not only had they scored twice, before poor Peter could get his breath back, but they had Jake so closely guarded that it was almost impossible for him to run with the ball, let alone get a shot in. Mr Ranson was not smiling now. With the score standing at two all, he was biting his nails with tension.

"Come on!" he shouted hoarsely. "Don't give up yet!" But he had to admit that a draw was much better than he had expected.

Yet, with only three minutes of the game left, his team mounted a last desperate attack. Just as it looked as though one of them might break through, Jake was brought down with a crashing tackle from behind. There was no doubt about it and the referee set the ball up on the penalty spot. Gavin Scot usually took their penalties and he came up now, ready to make the kick, but he had the reputation of being unreliable under pressure.

Suddenly the captain beckoned to Jake, "Come on, Jackson, see if you can make it a hat trick." Without any more fuss, Jake sent the ball into the left-hand corner of the net, right out of the reach of the disappointed Hurley keeper.

Not even at a Football Association Cup Final had any player been hugged more thoroughly than Jake was, when the final whistle blew and the team knew they had done it at last.

"Three beautiful goals!" gasped Peter, thumping Jake on the back. "I knew you wouldn't let me down."

The Hurley team, who once had jeered at Jake, now looked as crestfallen as their football coach, but it would have been hard to tell who looked more pleased, Mr Ranson or the Streetfield postman.

In assembly on Monday morning the Headmaster addressed the whole school.

"We have to congratulate our under-fifteen football team," he said. "On Saturday, for the first time in sixteen years, they beat Hurley School." A great rumbling roar went up from the school, but the Head held up his hand for silence. "The score was three goals to two," he continued, "and our goals were all scored by one boy, who played on the team as a substitute – Jake Jackson."

The enormous applause which followed reminded the confused Jake of a great fire crackling and through the sea of smiling, excited faces, he saw Mr Parker's furious glare. Jake's happiness was complete.

After that, Jake played every game. With Stephen Davson back in the game and Peter as goalkeeper, they were never beaten again that season. Mr Ranson's reputation was enormous in staff rooms all over the county.

Instead of the cries of "Red Skin" that used to follow Jake about the school, he was treated to respectful glances and near hero worship from younger boys.

Life was very good for Jake that winter, but his happiness did not last long, for his troubles were nowhere nearly over.

11

The Fire

The winter was mild and no football games had to be cancelled but, when March came, the weather turned wet and very stormy. It was about the middle of the month that the last of the puppies went off to their new homes. Only one remained, the little female they had decided to keep because of her lovely brown eyes. They called her Happy, in memory of her mother. Two puppies had gone back to their breeder, but from the sale of the other two the Jarvises had some money in their bank account.

"It'll be the first holiday we've had in ten years!" said Mrs Jarvis.

"The money we have won't see us through entirely," said her husband anxiously. "You boys will have to help me as far as you can."

Peter, who had a paper round, thought he might be able to get Jake a job there, too.

"I'll save all my spending money," promised Jake.

"No more smokes, then," said the little postman laughingly.

They spent each mealtime in friendly arguments about where they should go. Janie wanted the Lake District, while the boys favoured the sea. "But no cliffs, mind," said Peter, laughing. Mr Jarvis thought camping would be fun, but his wife longed for someone else to do the cooking.

"Jake ought to decide, really," said Janie adoringly, "because if it hadn't been for him, we wouldn't have had any puppies to sell." Jake just smiled happily and wished he could take them all for a trip around the world.

He only went to help Miss Potts on Sunday afternoons, now, for there was no further need for reading lessons and football took up most of his life.

"Time you started digging the garden for spring planting," she said one day when he had finished papering her sitting room.

"Time you started paying me wages," he said firmly. "I'm saving for me holidays, now."

"How could a poor old pensioner like me find the money?" she whined.

"They tell me you've got piles of money tucked away in here somewhere," he said with a grin.

"Oh, they do, do they?" she snapped. "I bet you'd like to lay your hands on it, wouldn't you?"

"No," answered Jake with dignity. "I'm going straight now, but I think you might pay me fair." Miss Potts opened her mouth to argue, but the thought of losing his company made her change her mind.

"All right then," she said crossly, "but don't expect too much."

Miss Potts's cottage belonged to Colonel White and she had rented it from him for nearly thirty years. He sometimes visited her to collect the rent and to keep a friendly eye on his old tenant. When he next stepped into the cottage, he was much impressed by its improved appearance.

"Well, Miss Potts," he said admiringly, "first you have the garden cleared and now the cottage has been decorated." And knowing what an old miser she was, he asked, "Who's doing all this work for you?"

"Never you mind," said Miss Potts in her own rude way and, going to the cupboard in the corner of her sitting room, she took out the polished mahogany box where she kept her money. The Colonel twirled his ginger moustache as he watched her rummage among the bills.

"You ought to leave that in the Post Office or a bank," he badgered her. "It's foolhardy to have so much money out here, miles from nowhere."

"Mind your own business," snapped Miss Potts, counting out the rent.

"I know all about that pistol of yours, but you never know where you are these days," continued the Colonel, undaunted. "Take that half-caste boy, for instance, the one the postman foisted onto Streetfield. He's got a terrible record, Constable Jones tells me. You can't trust people like him."

"Oh, I know he's after my money," cackled Miss Potts, wickedly. She meant it as a joke, but it cost poor Jake very dear.

It must have been the storm that woke Jake that fateful night. He had always been a light sleeper, but the wind that rushed around his attic bedroom and screamed at his dormer window was enough to wake the dead. Sleepily Jake slid out of bed, wondering if it was time for him to start his paper round. It was then that he saw the ominous red glow in the sky over the woods.

"That could be Miss Potts's cottage on fire," he

gasped and, pulling his jeans and jacket on over his pyjamas, he ran down to wake Peter. But he was unsuccessful, for Peter slept like a log and never moved until his mother attacked him with a cold wash cloth. Rather than waste more precious moments trying to rouse him, Jake gave up. He stopped outside his foster father's door, but it seemed a shame to disturb him when he started work so early. It might only be a haystack after all.

Out into the wind went Jake and over the fence. The woods, that he knew so well, looked angry and dangerous at night as the trees beat against one another in the storm. It was Miss Potts's cottage all right. When he arrived, he saw to his horror that the flames were already devouring her kitchen and the room above it.

"She sleeps over the sitting room though," he muttered, "so there's still hope for her."

The front door was locked. Diving through the smoke to the back of the cottage, he pulled the ladder from an outbuilding where he kept his gardening tools. It was rickety and riddled with woodworm, but it just reached Miss Potts's bedroom window.

The fire had been started by a hungry mouse. Half starved by the vigilance of the seven black cats, it had taken to gnawing the electricity wires in the cupboard under the stairs. Miss Potts kept all her old newspapers there, and the March wind blowing under the crack below the door was enough to fan the sparks into flames.

Miss Potts woke to find her bedroom full of smoke. She hobbled from the room only to discover that the staircase was ablaze. There was no escape and she knew it, so, calmly and without panic, she got back into bed and composed herself for death.

The sudden appearance of Jake's face at her window startled her considerably.

"Come on, you old fool," he shouted, putting his elbow through the glass and fumbling for the window catch. "Don't sit there all night!"

"I can't climb out of that window," spluttered Miss Potts.

"Yes, you can," answered Jake firmly. "And wrap yourself up or you'll catch your death of cold out here."

"Rude boy!" she muttered but, as she put an old red shawl over her shoulders, there were tears of relief in her eyes.

Then began one of the most nerve-racking experiences of Jake's life as, with great difficulty, he helped the old woman over the sill and onto the wobbly ladder. The heat from the flames scorched their clothes and the pain from her arthritis made her swear at him all the way down. But, at last, they were safely on the ground, and, taking her firmly by the arm, he led her away from danger. Together they stood sadly by the little garden gate and gazed at the terrifying inferno. For once the flames gave Jake no feeling of ecstasy, just a sorrowful knowledge that something special was going forever.

"My money!" gasped the old woman suddenly, "and my silver birds. I've got to go back in there."

"'Course you can't, you silly old woman," said Jake crossly.

"I can," said Miss Potts with energy. "The flames haven't broken into the sitting room yet." Taking out a key which hung on a string around her neck, she unlocked the front door.

"You can't go back in there!" shouted Jake,

grabbing her arm. "The wall might come down on you."

"The silver and that money is worth more than my useless old life," she said and shaking Jake off with one of her now familiar clouts, she put her shawl over her mouth and nose. The next minute she fought her way back into the house.

Jake watched her from the doorway, biting his fingers with tension as she pushed her way through the smoke-filled room. She knew her way to the cupboard blind-folded, so it took her no time to have the large box safe in her arms, but the silver birds were harder to find.

"Leave them!" choked Jake, but just then her groping fingers closed on her beautiful treasures. It was too late, however, and as she stuffed them into the box with the money, the fumes overcame her and she fell heavily to the floor, striking her head on the old iron fender.

The fire had broken through the door at the far side of the room now and a ghastly leaping glow lit the whole scene.

Without a thought for his own safety, Jake was inside the cottage and beside her. She was unconscious and blood was beginning to trickle from a gash on her forehead. Taking her by the feet, he tried to drag her to safety. But before the arthritis had doubled her, Miss Potts had been a very tall woman. With the best will in the world, Jake could hardly move her.

As he felt the fumes beginning to overcome him too, he did what he felt she would have wanted him to do. He snatched up her precious box and carried it to safety.

He had meant to dash up the path to the farm for

help, but when he reached the door of the cottage he ran straight into Colonel White and his cricketing nephew.

The gale had also wakened the Colonel and, looking out of his window, he thought that the woods he owned were on fire. He called the fire brigade, shrugged into his old army coat, and woke his nephew, who was visiting him. Together they hurried through the woods and arrived at the burning cottage at the worst possible moment.

"Miss Potts told me you were after her money," the Colonel bellowed, "but I never thought you would go to such lengths to get it. Hold onto him tightly, Mark," he ordered and plunged fearlessly into the cottage.

It did not take him long to drag Miss Potts out. He soon had her unconscious body covered with his khaki overcoat. When he had shut the front door, he noticed the ladder and the broken bedroom window. He finally took in the bleeding wound on Miss Potts's head.

Furiously he turned on Jake, who was still holding the box of money, while the nephew clutched Jake by his collar.

"Caught you red-handed, didn't I?" he boomed. "First you broke into her bedroom, then forced her to give you her money. As if that wasn't enough, you had to batter her brains out and set fire to her cottage to cover your tracks."

Jake's fierce pride prevented him from saying anything in his own defence, but his insolent silence infuriated the old soldier still further. Snatching the box, he brought his clenched fist smashing down on

78

the side of Jake's disfigured face. Through a fog of pain and rage the boy heard the Colonel add, "I'll make that postman sorry he ever brought a firelighting vandal like you to spoil the peace of our nice village. I've got some influence, and I'll see he's moved from this district immediately."

They tied Jake tightly to Miss Potts's gatepost with Mark's scarf. Jake hoped the burning cottage would fall on them, he hated them so much.

The woods were soon alive with firemen and ambulance drivers. When Miss Potts had been carried away on a stretcher, the local policeman arrived, panting, through the trees.

"We've caught the culprit for you!" shouted the Colonel proudly. "It's that half-caste of the Jarvises. You told me about his record for arson, but he'll go down for murder as well, this time."

Looking miserable, Constable Jones, who was a good friend of the postman, led them back to his tiny office in the police house by the village Green. Like everyone else in Streetfield, he was greatly in awe of Colonel White, so as they squeezed into the little room he sucked the end of his pen and looked harassed.

"I can only take statements at this stage," he said at last. "I shall have to have a word with my superior and see what the hospital has to say. We'll also have to wait for the Fire Chief's report before we can bring charges."

Colonel White snorted sarcastically as the policeman took down Jake's truthful statement and then thundered out his side of the story, incriminating Jake with every word.

Dawn was breaking when the policeman finally let Jake go, saying, as he opened the door, "Don't go to

school today, lad. My chief'll want to see you later."
Jake walked home down the lane, cold with shock,
his head throbbing from the Colonel's enormous fist.
His lungs and throat felt raw from the effects of the
smoke. But his feelings were hurt more deeply than
anything else. Wasn't it enough for the Colonel to kill
Janie's dog, without destroying Jake's world as well?

The postman had already left for work when he
arrived, but Mrs Jarvis and Peter were sitting at the
kitchen table drinking tea.

"Where've you been?" asked Peter sleepily.
"Hope you did my paper round as well."

"Whatever's the matter?" asked Mrs Jarvis,
jumping out of her chair as she caught sight of Jake's
extraordinary appearance.

She hustled Jake to a seat by the warm stove and
quickly poured him a cup of tea.

"What happened, love?" she asked at last.

"Miss Potts's cottage caught fire," mumbled Jake.
"I got her out all right, but the silly old woman would
go back for her money. While she was in there she fell
over and bashed her head. I couldn't pull her out and
Colonel White thought I was after her money and he
thinks I set fire to the cottage as well." Suddenly he
sat up very straight, spilling his tea in the saucer.
"You don't think I did all that do you?" he
demanded.

Mrs Jarvis thought wildly. She knew Jake wanted
money, and she also knew from Mr Lewis about his
deadly love of fire. She hesitated too long.

"You don't believe a word I've said, do you?" said
Jake in a strange tight voice. Kicking aside his chair,
he went up to the attic.

12

The Fugitive

The next two days were a nightmare for the Jarvises as well as for Jake. The house seemed full of police asking questions that Jake refused to answer.

Miss Potts's condition was said to be critical. She was still unconscious and suffering as well from shock and exposure.

Colonel White wasted no time in stirring the village up against the whole family and their lives were soon made a misery. There were no more friendly smiles for the postman as he went about delivering letters. One friend of the Colonel went so far as to set his dog on him. The little man thought himself lucky to get away with only a torn jacket and a hole in his trouser leg.

Peter had a terrible time on the school bus dodging a constant rain of missiles and abuse all the way to town. Miss Dixon led the women of the village against Mrs Jarvis, saying, with a contemptuous sniff, "I said it would end like this the very first day I saw that frightful boy!" When Mrs Jarvis went to the village shop to give her weekly order, the woman, who once had been her friend, said she had better take her business elsewhere, from now on.

Even Janie returned from school at tea time in tears because all her friends had suddenly turned into stony-faced enemies. Jake, hollow-eyed and silent, locked himself in his room, only coming down for meals. Even Peter could not seem to make contact with him.

Two days after the fire, the family was sitting around the table gloomily sharing the unpleasant experiences of the day, Mrs Jarvis's excellent tea almost untouched before them. Jake looked around at their worried faces and could stand the tension no longer. He needed the woods badly to be alone and free in them again, perhaps for the last time. But somehow he felt he could never face going to the woods again, so he had only the attic left.

When Jake had gone to his room, the postman said suddenly, "We shouldn't be sitting here like this. God said we ought to be glad if we got into trouble for doing the right thing. It doesn't matter what people say about us for having Jake here, when we know God sent him to us. So we're going to put smiles on our faces and eat up this good tea that Mum's made for us." The atmosphere in the room began to lift at once and they finished the meal in their usual cheerful manner.

Jake, alone in the attic, missed all that. He was feeling sick in his stomach at the thought of the misery on their faces. They would chuck him out now, for sure. Even if Miss Potts came around in time to save him from prison, the Jarvises wouldn't keep him. If they could believe he would do a thing like that, they would never feel safe in their beds while he was in the house. And why should they keep him and lose all their friends, as well as a job? He meant nothing to them, they didn't even get paid for having him.

As if to confirm his worst fears, he suddenly caught sight of Mr Lewis's car turning in at the gate.

That's it, then, thought Jake bleakly. The social worker had arrived to remove him from foster homes too many times before. Through his misery he heard Janie and Peter being sent into the sitting room to watch TV and the voices from the kitchen rose and fell ominously.

As he walked up the stairs to see Jake, some time later, Mr Lewis was feeling irritable. It had been a very long drive and it was supposed to be his day off. Jake had been a constant worry to him for years and when, only last week, he had heard from the Jarvises to say they wanted to adopt him, he had seen a way of being rid of Jake and his lengthy case notes forever. Now the Fire Brand had done it again. Those foster parents were so naïve they said they still wanted to adopt him and believed he was innocent, but Mr Lewis had known Jake far longer than they had.

When he opened the bedroom door and confronted Jake, the boy's stony, sullen expression did nothing to put him in a better temper.

He's a wrong'un, that one, thought the social worker. It's not worth wasting valuable time on kids like this. I doubt if he's got any feelings at all.

"Well, Jake," he began, "you're in trouble again and big trouble this time. I always knew it was a mistake to send you down here. These people are far too good to have been hurt like this."

Jake knew that was true, but all his old hatred and loathing for this man swept over him again and he shouted, "Get out of here, you Fat Toad!"

"Don't you talk to me like that!" spluttered Mr Lewis. "Or I won't lift a finger to help you in court. Not that anyone can help you much, this time," he added nastily.

"Get out!" repeated Jake and something about the boy's clenched fists made the social worker head for the door rather hastily and, stumbling down the stairs, he felt yet again that he had handled Jake very badly.

Jake stood in the middle of his room rigid with anger. Vaguely he heard Mr Lewis drive away and the Jarvises talking below.

A great choking wave of resentment and despair was breaking over him, and suddenly he was angry, angry, angry! First with his mother for deserting him as a baby, then with the many foster parents who had turned him out, with Mr Lewis for never caring, with Colonel White and Mr Parker, but most of all with the Jarvises who had brought him here and softened him up with this lovely room and the bicycle, only to turn against him when he needed them most. Suddenly he felt the whole world was a rough game of football. Everyone was bent on bringing him down into the mud. Every time he managed to struggle to his feet, they tackled him brutally once again.

"All right, then!" he said through clenched teeth. "See if I care." Tearing the football posters from the walls he crumbled them into a heap on the floor, together with his comics. He found some matches left from his smoking days and set fire to the heap. Then opening the window to make a draft, he stuffed his wallet into the pocket of his jacket and quietly left the house.

Smoke was already billowing out of his open window as he crossed the garden and went over the wall to the lane.

That old scrap heap won't take long to burn, he thought grimly. I always said I'd make that my last job here. But the thought of the house, where he'd felt so happy and safe, reduced to a blackened ruin, gave him a pain deep in his stomach.

He considered taking his bike, but felt he could not touch anything the Jarvises had given him.

If I cut over the fields, he thought, I can catch the seven o'clock bus into town and then get the train to London, before the police start looking for me. The money that he had saved for the holiday would buy his tickets and leave him some for food until he could start on a serious career of crime.

That's all they think I'm fit for, he thought, so I'll just have to show them how well I can do it.

He hurried over the fields, being careful to keep in the shadow of the hedge, for it was not dark yet. Glancing at his watch he saw he had plenty of time for the bus, so he paused on the bridge over the dam. Peter and he had spent so many happy hours fishing lower downstream through those long hot days of summer, but now the March storms had changed the river into a frothy brown torrent, surging over the dam. How easy just to jump! What did life offer him anyway? He would surely end up in prison wherever he went, with no woods, no football or fishing, and, worst of all, no Peter. Why not finish it, right here and now? The river thundered beneath him as he slowly climbed onto the parapet of the bridge.

The fire in Jake's attic had caught the curtains, and the flames were blowing back towards his bed when the Jarvises burst into the room. They had seen the smoke when they went out to shut up the chickens, only minutes after Jake had gone over the garden wall.

"I'll call the fire brigade!" screamed Mrs Jarvis.

"No, wait!" was her husband's odd reply. "I think we can handle this. Find all the buckets in the house and send Peter up here fast."

Braving the flames, he ripped open a cupboard in the corner of the room. Inside was the cold water storage tank.

"This'll save our bacon," he gasped, as he and Peter filled their buckets. The fire was safely out, but Jake's attic was a blackened, dripping mess.

"We're not telling a soul about this, do you hear?" said the postman, surveying the three other members of his family as they stood in the ruins of what had once been a bedroom.

"But he must have started this himself," said Peter miserably.

"'Course he did," replied his father. "But until I've had a chance to ask him why he did it, I'm not going to get him into more trouble than he's in already." The other Jarvises nodded gravely. "We'll just leave all this mess for the lad to sort out himself and he'll have to buy new curtains and wallpaper out of his own money."

At that minute there was a ring at the doorbell. Looking out of the window, Janie squeaked, "It's a police car, Mum." Guiltily they all went downstairs and found Constable Jones and Colonel White standing on the doorstep.

"Could we come in and have a word with you?"

asked the policeman.

"Surely," said Mr Jarvis, leading the way to the sitting room with a sinking heart.

"I had a call from the hospital, about five o'clock this afternoon," began the constable. "They said Miss Potts had regained consciousness and was asking for her landlord. They thought I ought to go along as well. Her mind was remarkably clear. She told us how your boy Jake had climbed up to rescue her from her bedroom window and risked his own life to do it. But she had insisted on going back in for her money. She remembers him trying to stop her, but after that her mind's a blank. All that was just as he told me in his statement," added the policeman, looking hard at the Colonel, who was strangely quiet for once. "She was worrying about the money, but when the Colonel here said the boy had brought it out safely, she sent us to thank him personally."

Colonel White had never been a man to shirk his duty, so, clearing his throat noisily, he added, "And I believe I owe the boy an apology. Apparently he behaved rather well."

"I'm sorry, but he isn't here at the moment," said the postman politely.

"Well, send him up to my place as soon as you can, will you?" ordered the old soldier. "I'd rather like to get this over quickly. I believe I also have him to thank for maintaining my cottage so well. All no good now, of course. Whole thing's burned down but, all the same, remarkable thing for a youngster to do and all for no financial reward, I believe."

It had cost the Old Man a great deal to say all that and his moustache was drooping badly as he got up to leave. "Miss Potts is much better," he added as he stood on the doorstep. "Giving the nurses a terrible time. I shall get her into one of the old people's flats on the Green and I'm having her cats cared for in the meanwhile." Feeling a little more like his usual self, he squeezed into the police car and ordered Constable Jones to drive him home.

"Thank God!" breathed the postman as he tried to hug all three members of his family at once. "A brand plucked out of the fire!"*

But their joy gradually faded as, hour after hour, they waited for Jake to come home.

"Stop prowling about like a tiger in the zoo, son," complained the postman, as midnight struck. Peter and Janie had both flatly refused to go to bed until they had seen the expression on Jake's face when he heard everything was all right again. But now the TV had closed down, Janie was asleep on the couch, and Mrs Jarvis had made so many pots of tea she had run out of tea bags.

"Something dreadful has happened to Jake, Dad, I can feel it," burst out Peter.

"Where's your faith, Pete?" asked the postman quietly. "Not two hours ago we prayed the Lord would take care of him; now we must trust Him to do it. Jake'll just be hiding somewhere, worrying about that fire he started upstairs. You go on up to bed, Mum and I'll sit up till he comes in." They sat up all night, but Jake didn't come in. Stiff and aching, they woke in their chairs as the clock struck six.

"Should we call the police?" asked Mrs Jarvis, as she warmed some milk.

"Give the lad until dinner time," answered her husband stubbornly, "and tell the children to keep quiet about everything in the meanwhile. The Lord's in control," he added and went off to work.

Zechariah 3:2

88

13

The End of Jake Jackson

The news travelled fast in Streetfield, that morning, and everywhere the postman went he was greeted by smiling faces and cheery waves. People congratulated him over their garden walls and from their bedroom windows. Colonel White's dog-owning friend even offered to buy him a new suit and said, "You must be very proud of that boy of yours. Fancy him risking his life for a terrible old woman like Miss Potts."

When Mrs Jarvis went up to the village later that morning, in search of tea bags, the very people who had ignored her the day before crossed the lane to shake her hand. The woman in the village shop came out to say, "I always knew that boy would turn out well. You've done a wonderful job on him!"

The only topic of conversation on the bus and at school that day was Jake Jackson's heroic rescue, and Peter ached for Jake to enjoy his hour of glory.

But when midday came and there was still no sign of the boy, Mr and Mrs Jarvis became seriously worried. "I'd better phone Constable Jones," said the little man miserably, as he pushed away his untouched dinner.

"You don't have to bother," said his wife, in surprise. "I see him just coming in the gate."

When the policeman heard that Jake had been missing all night, he looked very grave indeed.

"Mr Whicker's new cowman handed this in to me, just now," he said putting a shabby brown wallet on the cluttered kitchen table. "There's money in it, and your boy's name's inside. Ted worried all night, but he couldn't come and see me before, because it's market day. I'm afraid you'll both have to prepare yourselves for bad news. Ted told me he noticed the lad last evening, when he was on his way down to Long Meadow to fetch the cows in. He thought he looked a bit odd, standing on the parapet of the bridge, looking down at the dam. When he was on his way back with the cows, he found this wallet lying on the bridge, as if it had been left behind deliberately."

The postman's eyes widened with horror. "You think he may have jumped into the river on purpose!" he gasped.

"Well, he probably thought he was going to be charged with arson, theft, and murder. You can't really blame him, can you?" said the policeman miserably. Mr Jarvis dropped his head into his hands, but his wife was too shaken even to cry.

The police mounted a massive search for Jake. Inquiries were made about him all over the district, but no one could remember seeing him and, as Constable Jones said, "With a birthmark like that on his face, he'd never get far without being remembered."

So, frogmen searched the river below the dam, newspaper reporters swarmed about like wasps, and the stunned village of Streetfield began to fear the worst had happened.

Janie sat for hours at a time, with Happy clutched in her arms, staring dumbly before her. Peter could not pass the shed door for fear he would catch sight of Jake's bike, standing forlornly in the shadows.

Mr Lewis, in his London office, passed a nervous finger around his rather tight collar, realising he must have been one of the last people to see Jake alive. Colonel White sat alone in his great house by the Green, feeling much smaller than the little postman, whom he had always so despised.

It had been the thought of Peter that had finally stopped Jake from jumping off the bridge. Even if he went to prison, there was a chance he might see Peter again some day. So, blowing his nose loudly, he continued on his way for the bus. But he did not realise that his precious wallet had come out of his pocket with his handkerchief, and now lay forgotten on the bridge.

Nothing had gone right for Jake for so long that he hardly felt surprised to discover that his watch must have been slow. For, when he arrived at the road, he was just in time to see his bus disappear around the corner. It was a terrible blow to Jake, but it only slowed him for a moment.

If I go like mad and cut through the woods, I might catch it when it stops at the Rose and Crown, he thought. It oftens waits there a minute or two.

It was a slim chance, but he felt his freedom depended on reaching that bus, so he threw himself over the fence and into the woods beyond.

Of course he was running carelessly and far too fast and, had he been in his right mind, he would never have tried to leap that barbed-wire fence. One foot caught in the wire, and he landed agonisingly, with all his weight on the side of the other ankle. At first he was nearly sick with pain. Then the horror of his situation began to seep back into his mind. He could never get away now. He could not even move his foot, but his pride would not let him lie there and wait for the police to drag him away.

He looked about him wildly, like a hunted rabbit needing cover. Then he remembered the little ruined house. He and Peter had spent a delicious afternoon exploring its crumbling remains. They had thought it must have been part of the iron factory, like Miss Potts's cottage, but no one had lived in it for years. Jake felt sure it could not be far from where he lay. If he could only reach it, the old place might give him cover, until his ankle stopped hurting.

Crawling on hands and knees, dragging a broken ankle behind, is a very painful thing to do. When Jake reached his destination he was sobbing with pain, while the perspiration ran down his face. Biting his lip, he forced himself to crawl up the dangerous staircase, remembering that it was less damp up there than below. Finally, leaning his head on some old sacks, he closed his eyes and allowed himself to float thankfully away into unconsciousness.

The next two days passed ever so slowly for Jake, lying in his rickety hiding place. The pain in his ankle was intense, but cold and thirst soon began to trouble him even more. Fortunately the weather remained wet and he was able to catch the raindrops in his cupped hands as they fell through a hole in the roof. But that was only just enough to keep him alive. On the morning of the second day, he saw through a hole in the wall two policemen searching the woods near his cottage.

So the old woman's dead, he thought bitterly, and

they're after me, good and proper.

He had hidden from the police so many times before that he did not panic now. But he nearly shouted with pain as he hauled himself up into the old bedroom chimney. He did not really care if they found him or not, as he heard one say, "You go up there, Brown. Those stairs wouldn't bear my weight." But Constable Brown was obviously too frightened of the rotting floorboards to search thoroughly and Jake soon heard them leave. Should he call them back? He was desperately in need of medical attention. No. He'd rather die of thirst than give himself up. He ought to have jumped off that bridge when he had the chance. Why could he never do anything right?

His depression deepened as the day wore on. All his anger was spent now. He tortured himself by thinking of the Jarvises searching the smoking ruins of their home, looking for their charred possessions. How could he have done that to people who never did him any harm? Had little Janie got out safely? And had Peter been in time to rescue his guitar?

If I'd only managed to keep hating them, he thought, I wouldn't feel bad like this now.

It had been his friendship with Peter that had done it. He should have remembered that Peter belonged to another world, the real world, the safe world, where people were born into families – not rejected as babies and thrown away into the sea to swim for their lives on their own. No one really wanted people like that. Not "do gooding" foster parents, social workers, or God. It was a good thing he'd never made a fool of himself applying to God for adoption. Only nice, normal people like Peter, were suitable for God.

The little postman had always maintained that woods mend people, so that evening he took Happy and went off for a long walk, alone. The little dog had been much affected by the gloom in the house, so now she rushed ecstatically about, savouring all the delicious smells of the woods. But the postman could find no release from his grief and suddenly he felt desperately tired.

"Come on, let's go home, little girl," he called. But the dog was acting strangely, barking and pawing at the door of an old ruined cottage.

"Yes, there's probably lots of lovely rats in there, Happy, but we must get home now," said the postman wearily. But Happy, for once, took no notice of him. Forcing the door open with all her strength, she disappeared inside. With an irritated sigh, Mr Jarvis followed the sound of her excited barking, which came from the room above. He did not like the look of the worm-eaten staircase, but he was frightened she might have cornered some rats in their nest, so, cautiously, he went up after her.

There was hardly any part of the boy that Happy was not covering with her slimy kisses, but as Mr Jarvis picked his way over the treacherous floorboards, Jake turned his face to the wall. He remembered the way the postman had looked at him after the stink bomb affair and he had no wish to see that expression again.

It was typical of the man that he asked no questions, but just quietly sat down on the floor to wait for the dog to calm down as he took in the swollen, discoloured ankle and Jake's sunken, tortured face.

"Miss Potts is getting better," he said at last. "She told Colonel White how you saved her and her money, the other night. You're quite a hero in Streetfield now. Good job you popped out when you did, the other night," he continued, "because after you'd gone, your attic caught fire."

Jake turned his head then and said, "I done that."

"Well I guessed you might have, but I don't blame you," he added quickly. "You thought we didn't believe you about the fire at Miss Potts's and everything. But we did, you know."

There was a long silence and then Jake said gruffly, "I'm sorry I burnt your house down."

"Don't worry; you didn't," was the cheerful reply. "Peter and I had it out in no time. It made a bit of a mess of your room, but we aren't telling anyone about that."

"Why?" asked Jake, with a lump in his throat.

"Well, I don't want anything to hold up your adoption."

Jake looked up quickly into the little man's face.

"You may not want to be a Jarvis," said the postman, smiling. "But I'd be very proud to have the local hero for a son."

Jake had to look at the wall again, rather quickly, but he managed to croak, "I won't mind."

"Good!" said Mr Jarvis, and just to give Jake time to recover, he said, "We always wanted a big family, so it was a terrible grief to us to find we couldn't have any children. We've fostered lots over the years since then, but so far we've only been able to adopt two."

These words cut suddenly into Jake's tangled, reeling thoughts, and struggling onto his elbow, he gasped, "Peter and Janie?"

"That's right," said the little man, smiling.

"But I always thought – I thought they were your own."

"They are," replied Mr Jarvis indignantly, "very much so and probably more precious than if they'd come in the ordinary way. When Peter was two, his mother tied him to his cot and went away for good. I don't think he'd ever eaten anything in his life but biscuits and cold tea from a baby's bottle. He hardly weighed anything when he got to us. You wouldn't believe that, when you see the size of him now, but that's Mum's cooking for you."

"And Janie?" whispered Jake, whose world was turning upside down around him.

"She arrived so covered in bruises, sores, and dirt that she looked like that old doll Happy loves chewing. But she's safe forever now. Thank God."

"Why didn't they tell me?" muttered Jake, flopping back onto his sacks.

"Well, they don't really think about it much, you see. It's not important, really. They're Jarvises now and that's that. Same as you'll be soon, I hope. But we mustn't sit here yacking all night," he finished, scrambling to his feet. "I'm off to call an ambulance, now. Happy will keep you company till I get back."

When he had gone, Jake lay still, almost too happy to breathe. Adopted sons could never be kicked out. It was then that he suddenly remembered something.

"You kept your side of the bargain all right, God," he muttered, and struggling back onto his elbow again, he did what he'd promised to do. When he lay back again an enormous grin split his disfigured face in two.

"I'll be Jake Jarvis, soon, but I'm God's adopted son already."